Contents

Part 1

Introduction

The life of George Eliot

George Eliot was born Mary Anne Evans on 22 November 1819 near Nuneaton in Warwickshire. Her father, Robert Evans, began life as a carpenter, but by the time of his daughter's birth he was agent for the owner of a great country house, Arbury Hall, a position he had won entirely on his own merit. A man of famous physical strength, he was equally well known for his personal integrity and was master of an amazing variety of skills, from judging the quantity of timber in a tree to knowledge of coal-mining. Mary Anne was something of a favourite with her father whom she, in her turn, adored; indeed at the time of his death she said of her feeling for her father that it was the 'one deep strong love I have ever known'.* One result of their intimacy was that she received an early experience of the details of rural life from her father taking her with him round the estate on business. As far as is known, Mary Anne did not feel particularly close to her mother, who died when she was sixteen. The dominating emotional influence of her early life, apart from her father, was her brother Isaac, three years her senior. The childhood of Maggie and Tom Tulliver seems closely modelled on that of Mary Anne and Isaac.

In 1828 Mary Anne went to a school in Nuneaton where she encountered the first of a series of emotional and intellectual influences outside the circle of her family in the person of one of her teachers, Maria Lewis, who remained a friend for fourteen years. Miss Lewis was an advocate of a strongly emotional form of English Christianity known as Evangelicalism which placed a strong emphasis on self-denial and the avoidance of worldly pleasures. There were evidently aspects of Mary Anne's personality to which this made a strong appeal and at the age of fifteen she underwent a form of conversion similar to that experienced by Maggie Tulliver after reading Thomas à Kempis.† After her brother Isaac's marriage in 1841, she and her father moved near to the city of Coventry where she kept house for him. Despite her many household duties, she found time to continue with her unusually deep

*Gordon S. Haight, *George Eliot. A Biography*, Clarendon Press, Oxford, 1968, p.21.
†A religious writer (1379–1471), author of *The Imitation of Christ*.

and varied education, taking lessons in, amongst other subjects, Italian and German.

As a result of living near Coventry, she formed a friendship with Charles and Caroline Bray with whom she was intimate for the next thirteen years. The Brays were advanced intellectuals and under their influence Mary Anne discarded her extreme Evangelicalism, although there are signs that this process had begun before she met them. In 1842 she felt compelled by her conscience to take the extreme step of refusing to accompany her father to church. Robert Evans was a devout, if conventional, Christian and this refusal caused a breach that was never fully healed up to his death in 1849.

In 1844 Mary Anne began the first of her major intellectual tasks, the translation of *The Life of Jesus* by the German thinker David Friedrich Strauss, a mammoth undertaking that had already been abandoned as too difficult by several other qualified writers. The book was 1500 pages long and contained many quotations in Latin, Greek and Hebrew. Work such as this, and her friendship with the Brays, brought Mary Anne into contact with many of the leading intellectuals of the day. In 1851, for example, she began a friendship with Herbert Spencer (one of the founders of modern sociology) which might well have ended in marriage. The climax of this period occurred between 1852 and 1854 when Mary Anne was assistant editor of the *Westminster Review*, the leading radical and intellectual periodical of the day, which had been founded by John Stuart Mill in 1824. This time of relative stability had been preceded by a disturbing relationship with the magazine's editor, John Chapman. Chapman, who already had a wife and mistress living in the same house, was the centre of what can be seen as a recurrent pattern in Mary Anne's life, an emotional dependence which seems to have arisen from self-distrust. However, she appears to have extricated herself from this entanglement by the exertion of another, and equally strong, side of her personality, a self-control rooted in moral awareness of others.

In 1851 there occurred what was to be the major event in Mary Anne's personal life, her meeting with George Henry Lewes. Lewes was short, physically slight and, according to the wife of Thomas Carlyle, of 'immense ugliness'*, but he radiated an apparently endless amount of intellectual vitality and personal charm. He was also a writer of great variety: by 1850 he had published a 'popular history of philosophy, two novels, a life of Robespierre, a tragedy in blank verse . . . besides scores of successful periodical articles.'† He had been happily

*Gordon S. Haight, ibid, p.128.
†ibid, p.127.

married for eight years, but towards the e.1d of that period his wife began an affair with another man partly, ɛ ᵢ Lewes himself was aware, as the result of ideas of free-love which he had himself advocated. Lewes condoned his wife's adultery by accepting the son resulting from her affair as his own and thereby deprived himself of the possibility of obtaining a divorce.

By 1854 Mary Anne and Lewes knew that they wished to live with one another and took what was then the very difficult step of leaving for Germany as man and wife. Their action provoked a 'storm of horror'* and it is almost impossible for the modern reader to believe the insults, especially to Mary Anne, that were heaped on them. On their return to England, Mary Anne was forced to lead a solitary life, at least as far as 'respectable' women were concerned, for a very long time, although this had at least one positive result in her reading of Latin and Greek: 'This genuine knowledge of the classics ... was acquired during the long period of social ostracism when, because of her honest avowal of the union with Lewes, she was not invited to dinner.'**

In 1856 Mary Anne attempted some creative writing in the form of the short pieces that were eventually published as *Scenes of Clerical Life* and her career as a creative writer had begun. Over the next twenty years she published her great series of novels under the name George Eliot and it is hard to exaggerate the importance of Lewes as the encourager of what her lack of self-confidence often made an agonising process. The integrity of her life and the moral force of her work did at last secure her acceptance by society, although the forces of opposition can be judged by the reaction of even such an intelligent and sympathetic observer as Mrs Gaskell who could not accept that *Adam Bede* (1859), which she much admired, could have been written by someone in Mary Anne's position. She ended a letter to George Eliot with 'I should not be quite true in my ending, if I did not say before I concluded that I wish you *were* Mrs Lewes.'†

Mary Anne was prostrated by the death of Lewes in 1878, but revealed her emotional dependence by marrying John Walter Cross in May 1880, a marriage that re-established contact with her brother Isaac and her family, a contact that had been broken for all the years of her 'true' marriage to Lewes. She died in London on 22 December 1880.

*Gordon S. Haight, ibid, p.166.
**ibid, p.195.
†ibid, p.312.

The Victorian era

It is one of the pitfalls of historical writing to see the past as a series of periods of change and transition but, bearing this danger in mind, it does seem reasonable to claim that Victorian England underwent a constant pressure of extraordinary changes in the course of the nineteenth century. This certainly was the view of the Victorians themselves and the words of Uncle Deane to Tom Tulliver are representative of a great deal of contemporary opinion:

'You see, Tom . . . the world goes on at a smarter pace now than it did when I was a young fellow . . . It's this steam, you see, that has made the difference: it drives on every wheel double pace, and the wheel of fortune along with 'em'. (Book Sixth, Chapter five.)

The reference to steam reminds us that one of the most fundamental causes of change was the Industrial Revolution. The discovery and application of steam power had begun in the eighteenth century, but only began to develop its full potential during the period when *The Mill on the Floss* is set, the late 1820s and 1830s.

Perhaps the real significance of these changes in human terms can be brought out by stressing that they were qualitative and not merely quantitative. For example, methods of transport had been greatly improved in the eighteenth century—by road building and so on—and by the early years of the nineteenth century an extremely fast and efficient system of stage-coaches had been developed. The railways swept all this away and were not merely much faster; they broke a reliance on animals that had existed for as long as civilisation itself in favour of machinery. Thomas Carlyle, the great social thinker, saw his own time as the Age of Machinery and it does seem true that it introduced mechanical elements into human life where they had previously been absent. The stage-coaches had left on their journeys from London to Edinburgh, and the rest, at 'about' eight o'clock, or whatever other time was announced, as their advertisements put it, but the railways soon had timetables with their rigid and inflexible divisions.

This changed conception of time can be seen at work in other aspects of life. Industrial processes led to the concentration of work in large factories and this involved a movement from the land by very large numbers of people. (This, in its turn, led to the development of the huge industrial city, a new event in the history of the world.) From its very beginnings rural life had been governed by the time of days, seasons and the weather. Almost overnight, people whose lives had been governed by these rythms found themselves working to a rigidly disciplined day and week. The nature of work itself also changed under the pressure of mass production and the division of labour. An agricultural labourer's working life had consisted of a variety of tasks, depending on the needs of the moment. Again, a tradesman was used to carrying his job through to its completion, making his shoe or his chair, or whatever it might be. The large scale production of articles by machinery necessitated a factory worker's concentration on a single small task endlessly repeated, a momentous change for the psychology of modern society.

These are only a few examples of changes that occurred in the Victorian period, and if we ask how the Victorians themselves viewed them we get many different answers. However, when we remind ourselves how great many of the Victorian achievements were we should not be surprised to find that they are often very proud of themselves. Uncle Deane, again, can be seen as representative of an important strand of Victorian opinion:

'I don't find fault with the change, as some people do ... Somebody has said that it's a fine thing to make two ears of corn grow where only one grew before; but, sir, it's a fine thing, too, to further the exchange of commodities, and bring the grains of corn to the mouths that are hungry. And that's our line of business; and I consider it as honourable a position as a man can hold, to be connected with it.' (Book Sixth, Chapter five.)

But, as Uncle Deane indicates, others did take a different view. A great many social critics and, above all, creative writers did find themselves more or less seriously at odds with their own time. They objected to the immense human suffering that was connected with the Industrial Revolution, especially in the 1840s, and to the brutal ugliness of many modern cities. George Eliot can be seen sharing this view in a passage which connects Maggie's need for a higher life with the temptations of the poor to lose themselves in alcohol or religious enthusiasm:

'But good society ... is of very expensive production; requiring nothing less than a wide and arduous national life condensed in unfragrant deafening factories, cramping itself in mines, sweating at furnaces, grinding, hammering, weaving.' (Book Fourth, Chapter three)

There is nothing too unreasonable in seeing Karl Marx as a Victorian since he spent so many years working in the British Museum and, more significantly, used the English Industrial Revolution as the raw material for his theorising. He subjected the conditions referred to in the above passage to intellectual analysis, but a characteristic response of English writers to these conditions was one of emotion. And if we attempt a generalisation we might see the dominant thread in this emotional response as that of nostalgia, a widespread longing for a pre-industrial world. How far such a world was superior to the modern one is open to argument, but there can be no doubt that this longing occupied a significant place in Victorian psychology. In George Eliot this feeling was fused with powerful memories of her own childhood and the two combined seem to account for the artistic power of the opening chapters of *The Mill on the Floss*.

George Eliot and Victorian ideas

The life of the great writer seems often to have a significance beyond the purely private, to be somehow representative of major aspects of the life of his time. It is useful to compare Dickens and George Eliot from this point of view; indeed, a comparison between their lives and their artistry is one of the most fruitful ways of gaining an understanding of the greatness and variety of Victorian fiction. Dickens's experience of being forced to go out to work at the age of twelve gave him an insight into the economic realities of Victorian life, an insight based on the fact that his early experiences were typical of many in his own time. The representative nature of George Eliot's life, however, belongs to another area of Victorian history, that of intellectual ideas and religion, but it is as revealing of the inner life of the period as that of Dickens.

During the 1860s George Eliot's house, the Priory, became one of the centres of London intellectual life and if we look closely at the detail of her life at that time we see that she was often consulted by young men about problems of religious belief. These problems often had more than a purely abstract implication for it was impossible to be a university teacher at Oxford and Cambridge without being a member of the established Church of England, and so a crisis of faith could also mean the end of a career. People were drawn to discuss these difficulties with George Eliot because it was known that she had herself lived through the upheaval of a loss of faith, and so was well placed to comment on one of the central problems of her age.

We can see here another aspect of those changes which so many Victorians were forced to undergo. Men and women born and brought up in a religious belief unchanged for centuries suddenly found that the apparently secure foundations of their faith had disappeared overnight. Of course, to see the matter as dramatically as this was something of an illusion, but that was how it appeared to many contemporaries. The intellectual foundations of this transformation had been going on for many years in the work of German biblical scholarship; in fact, George Eliot had played her part in this process by translating Strauss's *The Life of Jesus* (1846) and Feuerbach's *The Essence of Christianity* (1854). Up to the beginning of the nineteenth century the Bible had been accepted as more or less an accurate historical record of the events it reported, but this biblical criticism showed that such a view was untenable, that if the Bible was to be accepted it had to be as something other than a factual account. For those who wished to see the story of mankind as beginning with Adam and Eve and going on from there this was a cause of acute distress.

If Christianity seemed to some to be weakened from within by biblical scholars, the best known of the external onslaughts was that posed by the discoveries of modern science. For example, work on fossils seemed to disprove the idea that God had created the world in six days, although one writer attempted to reconcile science and fundamentalist Christianity by suggesting that God had placed the fossils in the earth to tempt man to infidelity.* But the full impact of the implications of modern science for Christianity came only with the evolutionary theory propounded by Charles Darwin in his epoch-making *Origin of Species* of 1859. Twentieth-century Christianity has found ways of dealing with the problems posed by such a work, but for many thinking contemporaries it dealt a death-blow to the certainties of religious belief.

These were dilemmas, then, that George Eliot had lived through in her own life and with which, as one of the best educated intellectuals of her day, she was peculiarly well fitted to deal. We can best understand how George Eliot dealt with this problem for herself and something of why her advice was so eagerly sought by considering a wonderful letter she wrote in 1859:

'I have not returned to dogmatic Christianity ... but I see in it the highest expression of the religious sentiment that has yet found a place in the history of mankind, and I have the profoundest interest in the inward life of sincere Christians in all ages. Many things that I should have argued against ten years ago, I now feel myself too ignorant and too limited in moral sensibility to speak of with confident disapprobation: on many points where I used to delight in expressing intellectual difference, I now delight in feeling an emotional agreement.'

George Eliot was the best educated and most intellectual of the English novelists of her time, but these are the words of a creative writer rather than the abstract speculations of a philosopher.

*Edmund Gosse, *Father and Son*, Heinemann Educational Books, London, 1966, p.67.

A note on the text

The Mill on the Floss was begun in January 1859 and completed on 21 March 1860. The first edition was published on 4 April 1860 in three volumes by William Blackwood & Sons of Edinburgh. The second edition in two volumes was published on 29 November 1860 with few changes, but the one volume edition of December 1861 was carefully corrected by George Eliot. This became the main text for the fourth edition, made up of Vols. VII and VIII of the Cabinet edition of *The Works of George Eliot*. This was published in August 1878 when the author was deeply upset by Lewes's last illness and it does not seem likely that either of them read the proofs as they contain an unusual quantity of typographical errors.

There is no definitive modern edition of the collected works of George Eliot. Penguin Books are in the process of preparing an edition of *The Mill on the Floss*. Meanwhile, the best and most useful edition of the novel is probably the Riverside Edition published by Houghton Mifflin Company, Boston, 1961, edited with an introduction and notes by Gordon S. Haight.

Part 2

Summaries

of THE MILL ON THE FLOSS

A general summary

The novel opens with the author dreaming in her chair of Dorlcote Mill as it was thirty years ago, that is in 1829. The focus of her dream is a little girl, Maggie Tulliver, and as we move into the world of the book we find that Mr and Mrs Tulliver are discussing the education of their son Tom. Maggie is cleverer, more imaginative and, above all, more emotional than Tom, but she looks up to him with a love second only to that which she feels for her father. The novel's early chapters establish Maggie's dependence on Tom for her happiness and also create a rich sense of the way the Tullivers and Dodsons live. We see that Mr Tulliver, with all his good points, is dangerously ignorant of the world in which he lives, especially in view of his passionate temperament. Tom is sent off to an education totally unsuited to his abilities and position in life, and the stage is set for tragedy by a family disagreement which leads Aunt Glegg, one of Mrs Tulliver's sisters, to hint that she would like repayment of a loan she has made to Mr Tulliver. This difficulty could have been smoothed over quite easily, but Mr Tulliver's fiery temper makes him determined to repay the money although he is less wealthy than he seems to be to others.

We are given several examples of Maggie's naughtiness, such as cutting off her own hair, pushing her pretty little cousin Lucy into mud and running away to some gypsies. These events often arise from unhappiness caused by what she sees as Tom's harshness to her, but there is always consolation in the fact that she is the beloved favourite of her father. Tom goes off to school and Maggie visits him twice. She is fascinated by the world of learning, from which she is cut off as it is considered suitable only for boys. On her second visit she meets Philip Wakem, the sensitive and crippled son of the man whom Mr Tulliver thinks of as his principal enemy, and with whom he is involved in a lawsuit. Maggie becomes fond of Philip because she pities him and also because he shares some of his learning with her. Above all, she is moved by his thoughtfulness towards Tom when he injures his foot.

Maggie goes off to school with Lucy and when she is thirteen she is suddenly summoned home because of her father's serious illness, the result of his having lost his lawsuit and become bankrupt. Tom, who is sixteen, leaves school and immediately begins to take control of the family affairs. The aunts and uncles are willing to help, but Maggie is furious at what she thinks of as their harshness towards her father. Tom goes to work for his Uncle Deane, one of the partners of Guest and Company, and is determined to repay his father's debts. There is a plan for Guest and Company to buy the mill and make Mr Tulliver manager so that he will not have to leave his old home, but this is ruined by Mrs Tulliver's secret interference in going to see Wakem and putting into his mind the idea that he might buy the mill himself and have the revenge of seeing Mr Tulliver act as his employee, something he has not previously thought of.

Mr Tulliver recovers, agrees to work for Wakem and there now follows a period of dull misery for the family. Maggie is especially unhappy because her father and Tom are too preoccupied to return the love that she wishes to pour out to them. One day, in the depths of her loneliness, Maggie is visited by Bob Jakin who once worked for the family and who is now a pedlar. He gives her some books, one of which is *The Imitation of Christ* by Thomas à Kempis, and in reading it she experiences a form of religious conversion which convinces her that the only way of dealing with her present situation is by a course of complete self-denial, the willing acceptance of her life's limitations and the abandonment of her dreams of fulfilment. This causes a genuine change in Maggie and Mrs Tulliver is particularly struck by her new attitude, but we are made to see that this is unlikely to be a permanent change.

When Maggie is nearly seventeen she meets Philip again, and, although she has reservations about it, goes on seeing him secretly for about a year. Philip, who is in love with Maggie, introduces her to a world of art and culture which she feels she cannot live without, despite her years of religious self-denial. Tom eventually discovers their relationship, and, after cruelly insulting Philip, forces Maggie to stop seeing him with the threat that he will tell their father. Meanwhile, Tom has been working hard for Guest and Company and has also entered into a trading venture with Bob Jakin which allows him to repay his father's debts. On his return home from the celebration at which his creditors are paid, Mr Tulliver meets Wakem and attacks him in a fit of vindictive triumph. This, however, is too much for Mr Tulliver's weakened state of health and he dies the next day.

After her father's death Maggie goes off to be a governess, and we next see her at the age of nineteen when she has come to spend a month or two with Lucy. She meets Stephen Guest, who is Lucy's accepted suitor, although they are not yet engaged. Maggie still longs for a life in which art, learning and emotional fulfilment will be combined and she and Stephen are immediately interested in one another, although they do not immediately recognise this as love. Lucy wishes Philip to continue his visits to the house so that they can all enjoy music-making together, but Maggie feels that she cannot agree without first seeing Tom who is harshly unsympathetic at the thought of her seeing Philip again.

Tom has been such a success with Guest and Company that he is to be made a partner although he is only twenty-three. He takes this opportunity of raising with his Uncle Deane the possibility of the business buying the mill from Wakem and letting him manage it in addition to his other duties. Meanwhile, Maggie is enjoying a life of happy leisure, although she and Stephen are more and more aware of their feeling for one another. Lucy is unaware of this, but Philip's love for Maggie makes him jealously conscious of their developing relationship. Stephen at last betrays his feelings towards Maggie openly. She is outraged and goes on a visit to her Aunt Moss, but Stephen follows her and she admits her love for him. On her return to St Ogg's, Maggie and Stephen continue to see one another because they are convinced that they are going to part.

An outing to meet Lucy at a village on the river goes wrong when Philip is unable to row Maggie because of the illness caused by his jealousy. Stephen comes instead and, without Maggie's knowledge, deliberately allows their boat to drift past their rendezvous with Lucy. He tries to persuade Maggie to run away and marry him, but, although tempted, she refuses on the grounds of their old ties to Lucy and Philip. It takes Maggie five days to get back to St Ogg's on her own and Tom, who is now living at the mill, disowns her. Her mother goes with her to live at Bob Jakin's, and, despite being befriended by Dr Kenn the clergyman, Maggie is rejected by the community for what they see as her sexual misconduct. On the point of leaving St Ogg's, Maggie gets a letter from Philip and a visit from Lucy both of which assure her of their loving forgiveness. She also receives a letter from Stephen, begging her to marry him.

In the midst of this dilemma, the flood that has been threatening for days suddenly occurs. Maggie gets herself into a boat and is able to rescue Tom who is alone at the mill. They achieve a full reconciliation with one another and go in search of Lucy. Their boat, however, is overwhelmed by the debris floating down the river and they sink in one another's arms. The novel's conclusion shows that Stephen and Philip are still faithfully visiting Maggie's and Tom's grave five years later and hints that after many years more Lucy and Stephen finally marry.

Detailed summaries

Book First: Boy and Girl

Chapter one: Outside Dorlcote Mill

The novel opens by setting the town of St Ogg's in its context of river, sea and fertile countryside: the little town is an important trading centre for its neighbouring region. The narrator wanders by the river and looks at the lovely old Dorlcote Mill, noticing how high the nearby stream is and the evidence of flooding. As she looks at the mill wheel the narrator notices a little girl watching it also. Her arms feel numb from leaning on the stone bridge, but she wakes to realise that she has been dreaming about the past and remembers that she was about to tell us what Mr and Mrs Tulliver were talking about.

NOTES AND GLOSSARY
The opening alerts us to the fact of how directly the narrator is going to intervene in her own novel; this will happen consistently throughout the work.

The references to flooding form a pattern that helps to prepare us for the novel's climax.

Memory and a sense of the past are to be central to the novel's purposes.

Chapter two: Mr Tulliver, of Dorlcote Mill, declares his resolution about Tom

The Tullivers are discussing the education of their son Tom. Mr Tulliver wishes him to be something like an auctioneer, someone higher up the social scale than Mr Tulliver himself, who will be able to talk well and help his father in his business and legal difficulties. Mrs Tulliver's only concern is her son's physical welfare, but her husband is puzzled to know which would be the best school for Tom and decides to ask Mr Riley, a local auctioneer. They then speak of their daughter Maggie, aged nine, who is troublesome to her mother because of her habit of walking by the river and failing to look neat and pretty like her cousin Lucy. They both agree that it is a pity to have a girl who is cleverer than a boy, but it is clear that she is a favourite with her father.

NOTES AND GLOSSARY
eddication: education
be a bread: earn a living
Ladyday: March 25

Midsummer:	June 21
bit o' birch:	corporal punishment
raskill:	a rascal
vallyer:	a valuer
sanguinary rhetoric:	bloody talk (about killing birds)
spoke i' the wheel:	interfere
Holland sheets:	made of linen from Holland
mangled:	pressed
calkilate:	calculate
'cute:	acute, clever
Bedlam creatur':	a mad person (Bedlam was an eighteenth century mad-house in London)
mulatter:	a mulatto, of mixed European-Negro blood
gell:	girl
franzy:	frenzied, cross
Shetland pony:	breed of small horse from the Shetland Islands
patchwork:	cover made of patches of different coloured material
Raphael:	a famous Italian painter who lived from 1483 to 1520

Chapter three: Mr Riley gives his advice concerning a school for Tom

---

Mr Tulliver is consulting Mr Riley about Tom's education. He is afraid that without it Tom would wish to inherit the business and push his father to one side, but Maggie is indignant that her father should think any evil of Tom. She is then given the chance to show off her cleverness to Mr Riley, although he disapproves of what she is reading. Mr Riley recommends a clergyman as tutor for Tom, not from any precise knowledge, but from a complex mixture of motives.

NOTES AND GLOSSARY

cravat:	neck-tie
bonhommie:	(*French*) kindness
people of the old school:	old fashioned people
had had his comb cut:	Wakem had been defeated by Riley, a reference to attacking masculinity by cutting off a cock-bird's crest
Old Harry:	a name for the devil
weevils:	wood-boring beetles
Manichaesism:	an early religious system which saw Satan as co-eternal with God
Hotspur:	Harry Hotspur, a fiery character from Shakespeare's *Henry IV, Part 1*

oracular:	wise
Skye:	Scottish island
quarter:	three months
latter end:	death

I shan't be ... my teeth: I won't lose power while still active
akimbo: with hands on hips
The Pilgrim's Progress: by John Bunyan (1628–1688)
MA: Master of Arts, a university degree
curacy: a minor position in holy orders
feather out o' the best bed: that is, from the mattress
Ay, ay, Bessy, never brew ... poor tap: never make bad beer wherever it is brewed
a tincture: a little

Chapter four: Tom is expected

Maggie is unhappy because she is not allowed to go with her father to collect Tom from school. She goes off to a favourite hiding-place where she consoles herself by 'punishing' an old wooden doll. The weather improves and with it Maggie's spirits, and she rushes out of doors to Yap the dog. She shows off her knowledge of books by talking to one of her father's workmen, Luke, who points out that Tom's rabbits, which he had asked her to look after, are dead because of her neglect. She is once again very unhappy, but is consoled by Luke's taking her off to his cottage.

NOTES AND GLOSSARY
pinafore: an apron
fetish: a charm in witchcraft or magic
trunk: body
Jael ... Sisera: a biblical reference to Judges 4.1–22
poultice: dressing for a wound
Pythoness: a witch
auricula: powdery flower
au naturel: (*French*) unprepared, naked
shrill pitch ... mill-society: because of the noise involved
whipcord: thin, strong cord
offal: refuse, rubbish
gripe: pain
nash: nesh, weak
Prodigal Son: from the Bible, Luke 15.11–32
Sir Charles Grandison: character in the novel of that name by Samuel Richardson (1689–1761).

Chapter five: Tom comes home

Maggie is delighted by Tom's return and his giving her the present of a fishing-line. However, the pleasure soon turns to misery when Tom discovers that his rabbits are dead because of her neglect. Maggie retreats to the attic and eventually Tom is told by his father to find her. Maggie is forgiven and they have a happy fishing expedition the next day.

NOTES AND GLOSSARY

gig-wheels:	a gig was a light, two-wheeled, one-horse carriage
bowling:	movement of wheels
collar:	of shirt
croft:	small piece of arable land attached to house, small farm in Scotland
goslings:	young geese
physiognomy:	face
generic:	belonging to a class
phiz:	abbreviation of physiognomy
putting-up:	putting away
Samson:	a famous strong man in the Bible, Judges 13–16
lozenge-box:	a small box
whittling:	cutting

Chapter six: The aunts and uncles are coming

A family party is arranged by the Tullivers to discuss Tom's education, and there follows a celebration of the Dodson family with all its peculiar habits and conventions. Maggie is made unhappy by another example of Tom's selfishness and by his going off with Bob Jakin, the local rascal.

NOTES AND GLOSSARY

Easter week:	following Easter Sunday, the day of the Resurrection of Jesus Christ
lief:	rather
having:	greedy
allays:	always
beholding:	obliged
leggicy:	legacy
butter-money:	money earned by housewife for selling her own butter
nevvies:	nephews

offer:	try
leaves i' the table:	extra pieces inserted to make a table bigger
condiments:	flavouring for food
dry:	unbuttered
preserves:	jams
small-beer:	weak beer
impedimenta:	encumbrances
dubitative:	doubtful
bandy:	a game played with bat and ball
pudden:	pudding
rickyard:	an enclosure containing stacks of straw
Sut Oggs:	St Ogg's
rot-catcher:	rat-catcher
hollows:	shouts
yeads:	heads
Rhadamanthine:	from Rhadamanthus in Greek myth, a severe judge or master

---

Chapter seven: Enter the aunts and uncles

The family party begins with a conversation about clothes, illnesses, and so on, between the Dodson sisters. Because of the attention paid to Lucy's prettiness, Maggie cuts off her own hair. The family conference ends in a disagreement between Mrs Glegg and Mr Tulliver.

NOTES AND GLOSSARY

fronts:	false hair
tippet:	a small garment
chevaux-de-frise:	military defence work
smack:	a small sailing boat
brig:	a brigantine, a middle-sized sailing ship
Hottentot:	South African natives, vulgarly applied to savages
strings:	for fastening hat
asthmy:	asthma
hare-skin:	as a remedy for illness
boluses:	large pills
draughts:	doses of medicine
leghorn:	straw for hats, from Leghorn in Italy
tête-a-tête:	(*French*) in private
natty:	neat
Ajax:	a hero in Greek mythology
'half':	half-year, term

Lawks:	Lord (an exclamation)
niver:	never
spooney:	silly
wench:	girl
burning-glass:	a magnifying glass
constable:	a policeman
Lord Chancellor:	high government official, chief legal officer
yeoman:	an independent farmer
broadcloth:	good quality cloth
swinging:	high, strong
he knows ... to deal with:	up to every trick
bond:	legal document
craped:	black cloth
Duke of Wellington:	Arthur Wellesley (1769–1852), the famous victor of the Battle of Waterloo (1815), Prime Minister at that time
Catholic Question:	as to whether Catholics should have the right to vote
Blücher:	(1742–1819) a Prussian general at Waterloo (1815)
spelter:	zinc
Papists:	Catholics
Radicals:	reforming section of Liberal Party

Chapter eight: Mr Tulliver shows his weaker side

Mrs Glegg has threatened to demand immediate repayment of five hundred pounds which Mr Tulliver owes her, and Mr Tulliver, who is less wealthy than he appears to others, resolves to obtain three hundred pounds owed to him by his sister and her husband. But the sight of their poverty and thoughts of Maggie make him change his mind.

NOTES AND GLOSSARY

skein:	a quantity of thread or wool
dyspeptic:	liable to indigestion
plethora:	inflated (with blood), glut
murrain:	a disease of cattle
blight:	plant disease
father of lawyers:	a term for the devil
fallow:	uncultivated land
Markis o' Granby:	Marquis of Granby (the name of a public house)
guttered:	melted
Whitsuntide:	the seventh Sunday after Easter
prolific:	fertile in children

Alsatia:	a thieves' quarter in London, hence a sanctuary
arbour:	a covered seat in the open air
dressing:	manure
fortin:	fortune
thrums:	waste cloth from weaving

Chapter nine: To Garum Firs

Mrs Tulliver, Lucy, Maggie and Tom visit Mrs Tulliver's sister, Mrs Pullet, and Maggie is miserable because of Tom's friendship with Lucy. Mrs Pullet shows Mrs Tulliver her new bonnet and, while the children go out to play, Mrs Tulliver asks her to help in the disagreement between her husband and Mrs Glegg. The chapter ends with a startling sight.

NOTES AND GLOSSARY

musical box:	a box with a mechanism for playing tunes
coronal:	like a crown
tuckers:	material worn round the top of a dress
toilet:	dressing
card-houses:	children's game, building houses from playing cards
pagoda:	Chinese or Indian tower
bantam:	a small fowl
Guinea-fowls:	domestic fowls
brindled:	streaked
weathercocks:	devices that turn to show the direction of the wind
stucco:	plaster
semi-lunar:	half-moon shape
chef-d'oeuvre:	(*French*) a masterpiece
mollycoddle:	an effeminate fellow
Aristotle:	Athenian philosopher (384–322BC)
minatory:	threatening
cockchafers:	beetles
nincompoop:	fool
lozenges:	small sweets or pills
Ulysses and Nausicaa:	their meeting was an episode in Homer's *Odyssey*
milksop:	effeminate
horse-block:	to assist a rider in getting up on a horse
'fervescing:	effervescing, bubbling
pretty:	well
lawing:	going to law
scouring-time:	cleaning-time
pier-glass:	a tall mirror

Chapter ten: Maggie behaves worse than she expected

The startling sight is that of Lucy covered in dirt, the result of having been pushed in mud by Maggie because of Tom's continued friendship for Lucy and his unwillingness to allow Maggie to join in their games.

NOTES AND GLOSSARY

Medusa:	a figure from Greek mythology with snakes for hair and a capacity to turn people to stone
pike:	a large voracious fish
τι μέγεθος:	(*Greek*) greatness
Lors ha' massy:	Lord have mercy
corpus delicti:	(*Latin*) physical evidence of a broken law
spud:	a short knife

Chapter eleven: Maggie tries to run away from her shadow

Maggie decides to run away to the gipsies, but finds them frightening and wishes she could get home. Eventually, one of the gipsies takes her to the mill on a donkey and, on the way, they are met by Mr Tulliver. Maggie says she will not run away again and Mr Tulliver sees to it that her mother and Tom ignore the gipsy episode.

NOTES AND GLOSSARY

gypsies:	wandering race thought to have come originally from Egypt
commons:	unenclosed communal land
copper, sixpence:	coins
sleeves:	arm covering, then separate from other clothes
passengers:	travellers
donkey with a log to his foot:	with a piece of wood to restrict its movements
Apollyon:	the devil
highwayman:	a robber of travellers
fungus:	a growth such as a mushroom
shock-headed:	shaggy-haired
sphinxes:	colossal reclining figures in the deserts of Egypt
Columbus:	(1466–1506) Italian sailor, discovered America in 1492
Catechism of Geography:	question and answer text-book
Robin Hood:	a legendary English outlaw and popular hero who stole from the rich and gave to the poor
Jack the Giantkiller:	a figure in English fairy-tales

Mr Greatheart:	a character in John Bunyan's *The Pilgrim's Progress*
St George:	the patron saint of England
Leonore:	from Bürger's ballad *Leonore*, 1774

Chapter twelve: Mr and Mrs Glegg at home

The chapter opens with a description of the history of St Ogg's that reinforces the novel's concern with time and the past. Mr and Mrs Glegg are seen at home, their relationship is presented, and the chapter ends with her willingness to forgive Mr Tulliver and not ask for the immediate return of her five hundred pounds.

NOTES AND GLOSSARY

red-fluted:	a channel or furrow in a pillar
gables:	ends of a ridged roof
burthens:	burdens
classic pastorals:	Greek and Latin poems that present an idealised view of the rural past
bower-birds:	birds of the starling family
fatness:	fertility
Saxon, Dane:	ancient invaders of England
tumulus:	an ancient burial mound
oriel:	a type of window
Gothic:	applied to European architecture between twelfth and fifteenth centuries
trefoil:	the shape of three-part leaf
hagiographer:	writer of saints' lives
grist:	something to be ground
John Wesley:	(1703–91) famous preacher, hymn writer and the founder of Methodism
Dissenting:	refers to those who broke away from the Established Church of England
wool-stapler:	a wool merchant
slugs:	snails without shells
'contrairiness':	contrariness, liable to disagreement
out of a man's rib:	See the Bible, Genesis 2:21–22
blacking:	black polish
harrier:	hunting dog
Harpagons:	a character from Molière's *The Miser*, 1668
equils:	equals
weeper:	black mourning material
praeterite:	past

Chapter thirteen: Mr Tulliver further entangles the skein of life

Mrs Glegg assures Mrs Pullet that she will be friendly with the Tullivers, but the same day receives a letter from Mr Tulliver saying that he intends to repay the money in a month.

NOTES AND GLOSSARY
fervid: passionate
Oedipus: tragic figure from Greek mythology and the play by Sophocles, the Athenian dramatist (495–406BC)

Book Second: School Time

Chapter one: Tom's 'First Half'

Tom's schoolmaster, Mr Stelling, is a conventionally minded clergyman who puts Tom through the standard elements of the accepted education of a gentleman in this period, Latin and geometry. Tom does badly in his work and is pleased when Maggie comes to stay. She acquires some liking for Latin, but is disappointed when Mr Stelling tells her that women lack the ability to go deeply into intellectual matters.

NOTES AND GLOSSARY
snuffy: bearing signs of taking snuff
copperplate: a regularised style of writing
arabesques: ornamental lines
'my name is Norval': from John Home's play *Douglas* (1756)
Scripture: the Bible
Gospel: the biblical record of Christ's life
Epistle: a letter from one of Christ's disciples
Collect: a short prayer for a special day or occasion
percussion-caps: devices for producing a small explosion
supernal: heavenly
Massillon, Bourdaloue: French preachers, the first living from 1663 to 1742, the second from 1632 to 1704
evangelicalism: emotional form of Protestantism
diocese: an area under the care of a bishop
maltster: a maker of malt, grain prepared for brewing
'Swing': a form of intimidation against farmers and landowners
watered silk: material with shiny, wavy surface
Eton Grammar: a standard Latin textbook, originally used at Eton College

Euclid:	mathematician from Alexandria, who taught about 300BC. His *Elements* is still used, with modifications, as a text book in geometry
deaneries:	positions in the Church of England
prebends:	funds from cathedral for church officers
'mapping', 'summing':	drawing maps and making calculations
declensions:	grammatical forms
pointer, setter:	types of dog
Delectus:	passages for translation
supines:	Latin grammatical form
nodus:	(*Latin*) a knot, a difficulty
calenture:	a delirium
peccavi:	(*Latin*) I have sinned, admission of guilt
limbo:	a region on the border of hell
'first ideas':	philosophical term

Chapter two: The Christmas holidays

Tom returns from school to a beautifully described Christmas holiday, but this Christmas seems less happy than previous ones because of Mr Tulliver's increasing irritability over legal matters. He is annoyed by what he thinks is a neighbour's attempt to interfere with his water supply and believes that the lawyer Wakem is behind this.

NOTES AND GLOSSARY

fustian:	coarse
festal:	joyful
Puritans:	Protestants who disapproved of such things as Christmas celebrations
Old Harry:	a name for the devil
egg him on:	encourage
nuts:	difficult problem

Chapter three: The new schoolfellow

When Tom returns to school he discovers a new pupil, Philip, the crippled son of the lawyer Wakem whom Mr Tulliver regards as his enemy. Philip is sensitive, intelligent and very good at drawing, and he and Tom begin to form an uneasy friendship.

NOTES AND GLOSSARY

hump:	a deformity of the back
panniers:	baskets
'Speaker':	a book containing pieces for speaking aloud

David and Goliath: their battle is described in the Bible, Samuel 1.17
Richard Coeur-de-Lion: Richard I (1157–99) King of England, Duke of Normandy, and Count of Anjou, famous for his crusading activities

---

Chapter four: The young idea

Tom and Philip are constantly liable to irritate one another, although Tom begins to make some improvement in his education because of Philip's help. A general discussion of the difficulty of finding a good education for children in the period when the novel is set is followed by a scene between Tom and Mr Poulter, who teaches him marching. Tom's attempt to get Philip to look at Mr Poulter doing sword-drill leads to a bitter quarrel and the chapter ends with Tom persuading Mr Poulter to lend him his sword for a week.

NOTES AND GLOSSARY

Bannockburn: the site of a famous battle between the Scots and the English, 1314
satiny: like satin, silk fabric with glossy surface
Fortune: a Roman goddess
impromptu-phonetic: sound of words
circular: a leaflet
thumbscrew: an instrument of torture
divinae particulum aurae: (*Latin*) 'fragment of the divine spirit' from Horace, *Satires*, 2,ii,79
by rote: mechanically
Peninsular: the war of 1808–14 against France in Spain and Portugal
charger: a war-horse
Iliad: an ancient Greek epic poem by Homer
Bony: Napoleon Bonaparte (1769–1821) the famous French leader
General Wolfe: an English general (1727–59) who secured Canada for England from France in 1759
haction: action
Jupiter, Semele: in Greek mythology, Semele asked Jupiter for something that led to her own death, the sight of him in his true shape as a thunderbolt
mollusc: a creature with a hard shell
creosote: a wood-tar derivative used as a medicine in the nineteenth century
civil: non-military

Chapter five: Maggie's second visit

Maggie comes on a second visit to Tom and he injures himself by practising in front of her with the sword.

NOTES AND GLOSSARY

bovine:	ox-like
paternosters:	the Lord's prayer
comforter:	a long woollen scarf
Bluebeard:	the wife murderer of popular mythology

Chapter six: a love scene

Tom fears being lamed and, when Philip comes to tell him that he will walk properly, this leads to a reconciliation between them. Maggie and Philip become friendly, Maggie out of pity for Philip's deformity and Philip because he wishes he had a sister. They agree to maintain their friendship, but Tom and Philip gradually fall into a consistent coldness.

NOTES AND GLOSSARY

Philoctetes: a figure from Greek mythology who assisted in the downfall of Troy

Chapter seven: The golden gates are passed

Maggie goes to school with Lucy and she and Philip grow apart. As Tom approaches his last term, Maggie visits him to tell him that their father has lost his law-suit, is bankrupt and seriously ill. They set out for home together, leaving childhood behind and entering a period of pain and difficulty.

NOTES AND GLOSSARY

boarding-school:	a school at which pupils live
Eden:	paradise
turn-pike:	a barrier across road which is only lifted on payment
'fail':	bankruptcy
accoutrements:	equipment

Book Third: The Downfall

Chapter one: What had happened at home

We now discover in detail what had occurred at home. Mr Tulliver finds it difficult to accept the results of his failure and believes it will still be possible for him to go on living at the mill. In the midst of his trouble he feels a strong need for Maggie and sends for her from school. When he finally realises that his situation is critical, Mr Tulliver becomes seriously ill.

NOTES AND GLOSSARY

'It is precisely ... predominate still.': this is a good example of one of George Eliot's abiding themes, the tragic potential in humble lives

---

Chapter two: Mr Tulliver's teraphim, or household gods

The story resumes in the present with Maggie and Tom's arrival home. They find a bailiff in the house and Mrs Tulliver in the store-room examining all her household treasures. Tom is determined to help his mother by getting a job and this brings mother and son closer together. Maggie feels excluded, angry on her own behalf and full of grief because her mother and Tom seem to blame Mr Tulliver for what has happened.

NOTES AND GLOSSARY

teraphim:	idol, image of the household
bailiff:	a debt collecting agent
skewers:	for fastening meat
bailies:	bailiffs
chany:	china (cups, saucers and plates)

Chapter three: The family council

A family council is called to see how the Tullivers can be helped, but no one wishes to buy all of Mrs Tulliver's best things. Tom wins some admiration by his attempt to deal with the situation, but Maggie is furious because she thinks the family do not really wish to help them and because they all seem to blame her father. Mrs Moss comes to see her brother and the family try to insist that she and her husband should repay Mr Tulliver's loan of three hundred pounds, but Tom tells them of a conversation with his father in which Mr Tulliver said that he would never insist on having the money back.

NOTES AND GLOSSARY

unbagged:	dust cloths removed
head:	top
Homer:	ancient Greek epic poet
compendious:	concise

Bath chair:	a chair on wheels for invalids
draw:	pull
the parish:	a reference to the workhouse, an institution for the very poor
forrard:	forward
castors:	for holding salt, pepper, or other condiments
flock-bed:	rough, hard bed
yoke:	burden
physic:	medicine
codicil:	addition to a will
cupped:	taking blood for medical reasons
cumber:	encumbrance
assignees:	those who manage a bankrupt's estate
alienating:	lose or change

Chapter four: A vanishing gleam

The family's attempts to find legal papers rouse Mr Tulliver from his illness and he appears with all his old force. However, he relapses through anger caused by his thoughts of Wakem. The chapter ends with Tom's determination to destroy the evidence of Mr Tulliver's loan to his sister and to pay back fifty pounds to Luke, the Tullivers' faithful workman.

NOTES AND GLOSSARY

deeds:	legal documents
parchments:	animal skins for writing on
stroke:	an attack of paralysis
raskills:	rascals
sanative:	healthful
lesion:	damage

Chapter five: Tom applies his knife to the oyster

Tom goes to see his Uncle Deane, a successful businessman, to ask for advice in earning a living, but his optimism is weakened by realising how badly his education has prepared him for this situation. Uncle Deane continually presents Tom with the difficulties that lie before him and Tom leaves in a despondent mood which makes him behave harshly towards Maggie. We leave Maggie hurt at the contrast between reality and her dreams of happiness.

NOTES AND GLOSSARY

Tom applies his knife to the oyster: this is based on the saying that the world is our oyster, that opportunity waits for all

prosy:	dull, tedious
Practice:	method of arithmetic
themes:	school essays
Horae Paulinae:	(*Latin*, Pauline hours) title of book by William Poley (1815–88)
hair-powder:	for personal decoration
usher:	an assistant schoolmaster
unlading:	discharging cargo from a ship

he had not his port-wine before him: not speaking after dinner

rigmarole:	incoherent speech
round:	rung
pith:	vigour
bark:	outside of tree used in dyeing

nunc illas promite vires: (*Latin*) 'now put forth that strength', from Virgil's *Aeneid*, v, 191

Chapter six: Tending to refute the popular prejudice against the present of a pocket-knife

---

It is decided that Mr Tulliver should not be moved from the house on the day the sale takes place in it. When it is over Tom is asked for by a visitor, who turns out to be Bob Jakin. Bob has never lost his affection for the family and wishes to help them by a small gift of money that he has earned by putting out a fire. Maggie and Tom refuse, but are grateful for his kindness.

NOTES AND GLOSSARY

knocked down:	sold
'scrazing':	scratching, grazing

suffer a waste of tissue through evaporation: lose weight by sweating

tablets:	sheets for writing on
gen:	gave
squerrils:	squirrels
un:	one
scratter:	scratcher
istid:	instead
sharpness:	cleverness
drowndin':	drowning

jaw him a good un: talk him into it

niver:	never
ax:	ask
I sarve him out:	to pay him back, exact revenge
shy:	throw
raff:	riff-raff, low-class
nick o' time:	at the right moment
mantle:	cloak
pursuant:	following
'ear:	year
tentin':	tending, looking after
doused:	put out (fire)
suvreigns:	sovereigns (coins)
sperrited:	spirited
summat:	something
broth:	soup
chitterlings:	intestines
packman:	pedlar
chip:	bit
wescoat:	waistcoat
broke:	without money
penn'orth:	pennyworth, a small living
'quinetance:	acquaintance
nohow:	in no way
make-believe:	pretence
do:	swindle
flat:	slow-witted
flux:	flowing, discharge

Chapter seven: How a hen takes to stratagem

The sale of the mill draws near and there are plans to prevent the family from having to leave their old home. Mr Deane is considering whether his business, Guest and Company, should buy the mill and employ Mr Tulliver to run it as manager. Mrs Tulliver decides that it is time for her to act and she goes secretly to Wakem to ask him not to bid for the mill against Guest and Company. In fact, this had not occurred to Wakem, but he now decides that he will do so and keep Mr Tulliver on as an act of revenge.

NOTES AND GLOSSARY

lot:	destiny
taxing-master:	law court official
musket:	fire-arm

allocaturs:	legal certificates
Chancery:	the court of the Lord Chancellor
chain-shot or bomb-shells:	missiles used in warfare
ennui:	(*French*) boredom
Hodge:	a typical name for a rural worker
spencer:	a close-fitting jacket
eidolon:	a vague image
a priori:	(*Latin*) without considering the facts
erigation:	irrigation
pike and roach:	fish
sang froid:	(*French*) coolness
cockpit:	arena for fighting
jejune:	dull, dry
chiaroscuro:	shadowy

Chapter eight: Daylight on the wreck

Mr Tulliver is now well enough to go downstairs and the family are afraid of his response to the bareness of the house caused by the sale, as he is unaware of what has recently taken place. Mr Tulliver realises that he is bankrupt and promises his wife that he will work for Wakem.

NOTES AND GLOSSARY

crotchets:	odd ideas
'moithering':	worrying
'mushed':	crushed
Saturnalian:	referring to a Roman festival of complete freedom, even for slaves
Nemean:	Nemea, place where the Greek hero Hercules was reputed to have killed a lion

---

Chapter nine: An item added to the family register

As Mr Tulliver grows stronger it becomes more difficult for him to think of being Wakem's subordinate. On the other hand, he is deeply aware of the difficulty of leaving the mill with all its old family associations and personal memories. He and Luke agree in preferring the old to the new. Mr Tulliver becomes agitated and in the evening asks Tom to write in the family Bible that he will agree to work for Wakem, but will never forgive him. Tom promises to take vengeance if it is ever possible.

NOTES AND GLOSSARY

palms and banyans:	tropical vegetation
Zambesi:	a river in Africa
summat:	something
rust:	a disease of plants
firin' o' the ricks:	a reference to rick-burning, a form of rural agitation
malting:	preparation of grain for brewing
'ul:	will
'ud:	would
mysen:	myself
tow'rt:	towards
victual:	food
gripe:	cause pain
treadmill:	a form of punishment in prison

Book Fourth: The Valley of Humiliation

Chapter one: A variation of Protestantism unknown to Bossuet

This is a meditative chapter in which George Eliot discusses the spiritual limitations of the way of life represented by the Dodsons and the Tullivers, but in doing so she pays tribute to their practical virtues of honesty and hard work. The chapter also contains an important statement of one of the novel's central themes, the tragic potential of ordinary human existence, especially in relation to young people like Tom and Maggie.

NOTES AND GLOSSARY

Bossuet:	French bishop (1627–1704)
Rhone, Rhine:	large European rivers
glancing:	flashing
infidel strongholds:	a reference to the wars between Christians and Mohammedans for possession of the holy places in the East
emmet-like:	ant-like
chapel-goers:	Protestants who are not members of the Church of England
asthma:	a chest complaint
pall-bearers:	those who carry the coffin at a funeral
fromenty:	dish of wheat boiled in milk
Pitt:	William Pitt (1759–1806) a famous British Prime Minister
nidus:	place for seeds to develop

Chapter two: The torn nest is pierced by the thorns

We now have a description of the Tulliver way of life in their new situation. Mrs Tulliver is physically and mentally affected by poverty, Tom is increasingly silent, Mr Tulliver feels the constant shame of working for Wakem and Maggie feels a lack of response from Tom and her father to the love she feels for them. The men are determined to repay their debts and this leads the family to live as poorly as it can.

NOTES AND GLOSSARY

firing:	heat from house fires
incubus:	nightmare
pillory:	a place of punishment in which the head and hands are unable to move
sectarian:	see chapel-goers in previous chapter

Chapter three: A voice from the past

Bob Jakin calls to see Maggie one afternoon to make her a present of some books. Maggie feels her life to be utterly empty and is unconsciously searching for some way to make it endurable. She has tried to go on with her school work without success and this leads to a comment on the unsatisfactory nature of education for girls in this period. Maggie glances through Bob's books and is suddenly overwhelmed by one of them which teaches the necessity of avoiding self-love. Maggie's problem is linked to that of a society in which many have to work hard in unpleasant conditions to keep some in luxury and the point is made that a belief of some kind is necessary to make life tolerable for these suffering masses. Mrs Tulliver is amazed by the change in Maggie towards a quieter acceptance of things and grows fonder of her.

NOTES AND GLOSSARY

bull-terrier:	a kind of dog
sawney:	a fool
octavo:	size of book
cranium:	head
sot:	sat
banged:	beat
say-so:	very little
bettermost:	best of all
hev:	have
enow:	enough
skinflint:	miser

ferrets:	small animals used for hunting
varmint:	vermin
come over:	trick
Madonna:	mother of Christ
Burke:	Edmund Burke (1729–97) a famous orator and political thinker
pricked:	rode (horse)
Télemaque:	novel by Fénelon (1651–1715), published in 1699
bran:	the inner husk of corn
Smithfield:	site in London of execution of religious martyrs
Christian Year:	a book by J. Keble (1792–1866), published in 1827
Thomas à Kempis:	religious writer (1379–1471)
vortices:	swirling masses
Faraday:	Michael Faraday (1791–1867), a well known British scientist
ekstasis:	ecstasy

Book Fifth: Wheats and Tares

Chapter one: In the Red Deeps

Maggie sees Philip again, but avoids a meeting with him. However, Philip lies in wait for her on a favourite walk as he is determined to resume their acquaintance. Philip shows Maggie a portrait he painted of her as she looked when they last met. It is obvious that he is in love with her and equally obvious that Maggie feels nothing more than warm friendship for him. Against her better judgement, Maggie allows Philip to persuade her to let him see her again.

NOTES AND GLOSSARY

tares:	weeds in a cornfield
ampitheatre:	here level ground surrounded by rising slopes
faëry:	old word for fairy, imaginary world
'avaunt':	go away

Chapter two: Aunt Glegg learns the breadth of Bob's thumb

Tom is beginning to please his relatives by his steady application to business, although he finds the attempt to save enough to repay his father's debts very slow work. Bob Jakin re-appears with a scheme to invest money in trading which seems likely to help Tom to get on faster. Mr Tulliver is reluctant to risk their joint savings and so Tom goes for help to his Uncle Glegg. After a comic interlude in which Bob tricks Mrs Glegg into buying some goods, the Gleggs agree to finance Tom.

NOTES AND GLOSSARY

Hecuba:	in Greek legend, the wife of King Priam of Troy
Hector:	a son of Priam and Hecuba
excursus:	digression
execution:	carrying out of legal formalities
speak without book:	without thought
zent:	cent
carguy:	cargo
passill:	parcel
shupercargo:	supercargo, agent in charge of cargo on board ship
Aaron:	The source is biblical, Exodus 4.14–16,30
nephey:	nephew
'sizes:	assizes, periodical sitting of judges
hish:	hiss
newfangled:	modern
stock:	collar
faitures:	features
imperent:	impudent
fortin:	fortune
a soft:	a fool
net:	material, especially for veils
a junketing:	a good time
hankicher:	a handkerchief
thack:	thatch
Victoree:	Victoria
buff:	light brownish yellow colour
vally:	value
vibs:	lies
Catechism:	treatise for Christian instruction

Chapter three: The wavering balance

Maggie is determined that she and Philip should stop seeing one another, but Philip feels that she is wasting her life by refusing to have contact with culture and the great outside world through him. He persuades Maggie that they should go on meeting as if by chance.

NOTES AND GLOSSARY

fleckered:	marked by flecks
Hamadryad:	a wood-nymph in Greek legend

Chapter four: Another love scene

Almost a year has passed and it is clear that Maggie and Philip have been meeting regularly. Philip cannot resist letting Maggie know that he loves her and this comes as a complete surprise to her. In response to his persistence, she admits to thinking that she could not love any one better than him and the chapter ends with Maggie's sense that she is sacrificing herself in loving him.

NOTES AND GLOSSARY

rolls: of sheet music
Rebecca . . . : these are fictional characters
woof: woven fabric, texture

Chapter five: The cloven tree

Maggie's great fear has been that her secret relationship with Philip will be discovered. A chance remark by Aunt Pullet causes Maggie such embarrassment that Tom is made suspicious and he traps her as she is about to meet Philip. He forces her to give Philip up by threatening to expose the relationship to their father. Tom then accompanies Maggie to her meeting with Philip and, while accusing him of playing with Maggie's affections, brutally insults his physical deformity. Despite all her unhappiness, Maggie, in being forced to separate from Philip, feels a certain relief that she is unable to understand.

NOTES AND GLOSSARY

tasty: tasteful
yallow: yellow
bell: belle, beauty
Pharisee: a self-righteous person

Chapter six: The hard-won triumph

Tom returns home from work unexpectedly early in a state of suppressed excitement and asks his father to count their savings. Mr Tulliver is depressed at the thought of how far they still have to go to repay his debts, but Tom is able to produce the required amount, the fruit of his trading venture with Bob Jakin. The family is overjoyed to learn that a meeting has been arranged at which all the creditors are to be paid.

NOTES AND GLOSSARY

A change into the present tense in the chapter's opening paragraph serves to heighten the excitement of its dramatic event.

Chapter seven: A day of reckoning

The satisfaction of the meeting to pay off the debts, at which Tom is praised by all, ends in tragedy. Mr Tulliver meets Wakem on his way home, and, in a state of wild triumph, causes Wakem to fall from his horse and beats him. Maggie stops her father and he is thrown into a state of exhaustion by these events. His condition worsens in the night and he dies in the morning. Maggie begs Tom's forgiveness and they sorrow together.

Book Sixth: The Great Temptation

Chapter one: A duet in paradise

Maggie's cousin Lucy is talking confidentially with Stephen Guest, the son of the leading partner in Guest and Company, and we learn that Maggie has been teaching at a school for the past two years. She is about to come on holiday to see Lucy whose mother is dead and whose house is looked after by Mrs Tulliver. Lucy and Stephen are evidently in love, although they are not yet engaged, and it is clear that Stephen patronises Lucy a little. Both are afraid that their music making will be spoiled by Maggie's unwillingness to meet Philip, who sings with them. Lucy decides not to correct Stephen's impression that Maggie will look like her mother.

NOTES AND GLOSSARY

'King Charles':	a type of spaniel dog
attar of roses:	perfume
odoriferous:	perfumed
da capo:	(*Italian*) from the beginning
ratafias:	kind of biscuits
buckram:	dress material
roundrobin:	circular letter
Lucifer:	chief of the fallen angels, see the Bible, Isaiah 14.12
Turpin:	a highwayman, famous as a rider (1706–39)
The Creation:	by Haydn (1732–1809)
Adam and Eve:	see the Bible, Genesis 2–4
fugue:	a musical form
rotten boroughs:	areas which sent members to Parliament without a real basis of voters, reformed by Bill of 1831–3
Raphael:	an archangel

chiffonier: piece of furniture with drawers for odds and ends
'the more familiar rodents': mice
Judas: Judas Iscariot, the betrayer of Jesus Christ

Chapter two: First impressions

Maggie and Lucy are talking of Stephen, although Maggie finds it difficult to shake off the depressing memories of her school life. Lucy is determined to give her a holiday full of pleasure. Left alone, Maggie is conscious of how far she has moved from her old ideal of renouncing happiness and contentedly bearing a dull life. Stephen enters and is overcome with astonished embarrassment at Maggie's appearance. He finds himself interested by the fact that Maggie does not respond to his easy compliments. Mention is made of Dr Kenn, the local clergyman, and his acts of charity, and Maggie is delighted to be taken rowing with Lucy by Stephen.

NOTES AND GLOSSARY
aerial: slight
merino: soft woollen material
Cinderella: the badly treated heroine of a fairy story
alumnus: student
Purcell: (1659–95), an English composer of music

Chapter three: Confidential moments

Maggie is in her bedroom but unable to sleep after the excitement of music. Lucy enters for a late chat and frightens Maggie by telling her that Philip will be coming tomorrow. Maggie says that she will see Tom and tell him that Lucy wishes Philip to come to the house. Finally, under the influence of Lucy's affectionate interest, Maggie tells her of her relationship with Philip, although she seems somehow upset at Lucy's plan that Maggie and Philip should marry at the same time as she and Stephen.

NOTES AND GLOSSARY
Sir Andrew Aguecheek: a character in Shakespeare's *Twelfth Night*

Chapter four: Brother and sister

Maggie visits Tom, who now lives with Bob Jakin and his wife, and is saddened by the contrast between his present life and the home they knew together. Bob tells Maggie of his worries about Tom and she realises that he may be in love with Lucy. Tom is harsh in response to Maggie's desire to see Philip and says that he cannot trust her. Maggie recognises some truth in Tom's view of her, but feels that he never tries to understand her from the inside. However, they are able to part affectionately.

NOTES AND GLOSSARY

taters:	potatoes
biler:	boiler
'cutish:	acute, clever
worrets:	worries
glumpish:	gloomy

Chapter five: Showing that Tom had opened the oyster

Tom keeps an appointment with his Uncle Deane who begins by talking of the fast pace of modern life which he attributes to steam power. Mr Deane announces that he and Mr Guest wish to reward Tom for his services by making him a partner in the firm. Tom responds by hoping that the firm will buy Dorlcote Mill from Wakem and put him in as manager.

Chapter six: Illustrating the laws of attraction

Maggie is enjoying a life of unaccustomed leisure in which she has nothing to do but enjoy the beauties of life and be made a fuss of. Lucy is pleased at how well Maggie and Stephen get on together and is unaware of a feeling between them which they do not admit to themselves. Maggie is left alone one evening and Stephen makes an unexpected visit which is clearly not accidental and which embarrasses them both. He persuades Maggie to walk round the garden with him; she suddenly breaks away and rushes into the house to cry while Stephen spends the evening thoroughly annoyed at his own behaviour.

NOTES AND GLOSSARY

gaucherie:	(*French*) awkwardness
Novalis:	a German author (1772–1801)
Miss Sophia Western:	a character in Henry Fielding's (1707–54) novel *Tom Jones* (1749)
reticules:	small bags
cribbage:	a card game, the score in which is kept by pegs in a board
pool:	a game played on a billiard table

Chapter seven: Philip re-enters

Maggie meets Philip again in a moment of painful happiness for both. From the beginning Philip suspects a change in Maggie and this is strengthened by his perception of an awareness between Maggie and Stephen. Lucy discovers that her father is interested in Guest and Company buying Dorlcote Mill and she persuades him to allow her to discuss the problem with Philip.

NOTES AND GLOSSARY

mackintosh:	waterproof coat
canterbury:	a stand for holding music
'Somnambula':	an opera by Bellini (1803–35)
bobbins:	used in sewing
accompt:	account

Chapter eight: Wakem in a new light

Philip asks his father to come to his studio to look at his sketches and Mr Wakem is angered by seeing two portraits of Maggie. Philip tells him that he loves her, but that he realises that he can only marry with his father's consent as he could not offer Maggie poverty as well as his deformity. Their conversation is resumed after a break and Mr Wakem, moved by memories of his wife and pain for Philip's condition, agrees to give his consent and to sell the mill to Guest and Company.

NOTES AND GLOSSARY
In a way highly characteristic of George Eliot we are made to see in this chapter that even Mr Wakem has a finer side to his character than we had realised.

Chapter nine: Charity in full dress

Maggie has a triumph at the bazaar because of the refined simplicity of her beauty. Stephen sees Mr Wakem buying something from her and then feels forced to talk to her although he has been trying to keep away. Maggie begs him to go and Stephen becomes aware that Philip is looking at them. He tells Philip that he can never please Maggie, but Philip angrily accuses him of hypocrisy. Maggie is upset by her encounter with Stephen and feels a brief bond of friendship with Dr Kenn because of his sympathy. Lucy is very unhappy when Maggie tells her that she is soon going away to another teaching position and cannot marry Philip because of her relationship with Tom.

NOTES AND GLOSSARY

bazaar:	a fair for selling small articles
heraldic:	referring to devices to represent noble families
seigniors:	those of high rank
orchestra:	large space in a building
Caucasus:	an area of Russia noted for its cold weather
forte:	strong point
Python:	in Greek mythology the monster killed near Delphi by Apollo
Correggio:	(1489–1534) Italian painter famous for religious subjects

Chapter ten: The spell seems broken

Maggie goes to a dance at Stephen's home and eventually allows herself to enjoy an old country-dance, although she refuses to join in the modern dances. Stephen eventually asks her to walk with him and they go into the conservatory. He cannot resist kissing Maggie's arm and she is filled with anger and a sense of betrayal towards Lucy which helps her to feel that her relationship with Stephen is now over. Philip calls the next morning and she tells him that it is only her feeling for Tom that could keep them always apart.

NOTES AND GLOSSARY

caps:	women's head-dress
conservatory:	a heated room for flowers and plants

Chapter eleven: In the lane

Maggie goes to stay with her Aunt Moss. Stephen appears unexpectedly in an obviously distraught condition and asks her to walk with him. Stephen tries to persuade Maggie that it is right for them to marry, but she can only see this as a betrayal of older ties. She tells Stephen that she loves him, they kiss and then part.

NOTES AND GLOSSARY

avatar:	god-like figure

Chapter twelve: A family party

A family party is held at Aunt Pullet's to celebrate the Tullivers' return to the mill and the sisters agree to give Mrs Tulliver some of their things with which to start up house again. Lucy travels with Tom on her way home and explains to him the part played by Philip in regaining the mill. Instead of the positive response she had expected, Tom merely says that he would never give his approval to Maggie's marriage to Philip.

NOTES AND GLOSSARY

millenium:	period of future happiness
cockatrices:	mythological serpents
Indy:	Indian
muffineer:	for sprinkling salt or sugar on muffins, a form of toasted cake

Chapter thirteen: Borne along by the tide

Maggie returns to St Ogg's and she and Stephen see each other every evening despite his resolve to go away. Both feel this is justified because they are soon to part. Lucy arranges a plan whereby she is to travel to a village on the river with her father where they will be met by Maggie and Philip who will boat there. However, Philip is so upset by observing the relationship between Maggie and Stephen that he is unable to go out. Stephen comes to Maggie instead and, against her better judgement, persuades her to let him row her. Stephen allows their boat to drift past the appointed village and it is late when Maggie realises what has happened. Stephen suggests that they travel to Scotland to marry, but Maggie is indignant at this. They are taken on to a passing trading-ship and Maggie falls asleep full of the pleasure of the moment.

NOTES AND GLOSSARY

locomotion:	method of travel

Chapter fourteen: Waking

Maggie wakes and feels that they have committed a great error. When they reach land she tells Stephen that they must part. They go to an inn and Stephen argues that it is right for them to stay together, but Maggie responds that it cannot be correct for them to build their happiness on the misery of others. Filled with agony at her refusal to marry him, Stephen tells Maggie to go and she begins the long journey home.

NOTES AND GLOSSARY

tarpauling:	tarpaulin, canvas cover
Virgin:	Mary, the mother of Jesus Christ

Book Seventh: The Final Rescue

Chapter one: The return to the mill

Tom is standing outside the mill on the fifth day after Maggie's and Stephen's disappearance, his happiness in having recovered the mill turned to bitterness by his sister's behaviour. Maggie appears to beg forgiveness, but Tom tells her that she no longer belongs to him. He will support her, but she cannot live at the mill. Maggie is joined by her mother and they go to stay at Bob Jakin's. Bob tries to comfort Maggie by bringing his baby to her and she asks him to go for Dr Kenn. However, Dr Kenn's wife has just died and so he cannot be disturbed.

NOTES AND GLOSSARY
the warmest department of an asylum: hell
leather: beat, thrash
arter: afterwards
make no jaw: keep quiet

Chapter two: St Ogg's passes judgement

We now have a description, in its own words, of what St Ogg's would have thought if Maggie and Stephen had married and returned after a few months. This contrasts favourably with the actual response to Maggie's giving Stephen up. A week later a letter comes to his father from Stephen, who is in Holland, explaining exactly what happened between him and Maggie. Maggie is in agony to know how Lucy (who has been very ill) and Philip are. She begins to do some sewing in order to earn her living and eventually is able to see Dr Kenn. He believes in Maggie but thinks it best that she should go away. However, he gives way in the face of her insistence that she must stay in St Ogg's.

NOTES AND GLOSSARY
trousseau: (*French*) wedding outfit
will put up for the borough: stand for election as a Member of Parliament
physique: (*French*) physical presence
nonchalance: (*French*) ease of manner
imbruted: brutalised
schismatics: Protestants who are not members of the established Church of England
I should have no stay: I should have no support
casuists: those who deal with moral problems in an evasive way
maxims: rules or principles of conduct

Chapter three: Showing that old acquaintances are capable of surprising us

Mrs Glegg is surprisingly revealed as one of Maggie's supporters. She believes that it is a family duty to help Maggie unless she is proved to be bad. However, she is unable to persuade Tom to take Maggie back into the mill. Maggie receives a letter from Philip which amounts to a justification of her decision not to marry Stephen. In it he assures Maggie of his complete faith in her and of the fact that his love for her had led him into a fuller life than he could have believed possible for him.

NOTES AND GLOSSARY

legatee: one to whom something has been left in a will
extry: extra

Chapter four: Maggie and Lucy

Dr Kenn is shocked by the persistent opposition to Maggie and decides that the only way to help her is to employ her to look after his children. This immediately starts rumours that Maggie is trying to trap Dr Kenn into marriage. Maggie hears that Lucy is to go to the sea-side in an attempt to recover and longs to see her. Just before her departure, Lucy comes secretly to see Maggie and they are able to take a loving farewell of one another.

NOTES AND GLOSSARY

Peter: the disciple who briefly denied Christ, see the Bible, Luke 22.56–62

Chapter five: The last conflict

Maggie is sitting alone at night while a rain storm rages outside. She has had to give up going to Dr Kenn's because of the gossip about them and feels utterly lonely as Dr Kenn has told her that he thinks that she must really go away from St Ogg's. She has had a letter from Stephen, who has returned secretly from abroad, in which he begs her to marry him. Maggie is tempted by this prospect of happiness but, as she prays for strength to resist it, she is suddenly aware of water flooding into the house. She and Bob each get into a boat and Maggie finds herself carried away on the current. Gradually she is able to get to the mill and rescue Tom who is alone there. As they gaze at one another in the boat, Tom can see that Maggie is innocent and the breach between them is healed. They go in search of Lucy, but are overwhelmed by a mass of floating débris and sink in a final embrace.

Conclusion

Five years have passed. Maggie and Tom are buried together in a grave that is often visited by Stephen and Philip. We are given a hint that many years later Stephen and Lucy marry.

NOTES AND GLOSSARY
'In their death . . . divided': see the Bible, 2 Samuel, 1.23

Part 3

Commentary

Artistry

Plot

This is an area where, as was suggested earlier, it is possible to make an instructive comparison between George Eliot and Dickens. The plots of Dickens's later novels are immensely complex and are often dependent on the solution of a mystery. For example, in *Great Expectations* the question of the origins of Pip's money is not only crucial to the working out of the story but part of the final meaning of the book. In other words, plot and meaning are inseperably connected. *The Mill on the Floss* clearly does not work in this way. Its unravelling of events is quite straightforward and free from mysteries of any external kind. George Eliot's attitude to plot can be seen in the novel's handling of time, which leaps forward over a period of years on several occasions. The development of a complex and connected series of events is not central to the artistry of this novel.

To say this is not to depreciate George Eliot's skills but to emphasise the things which particularly interest her. All novels are concerned with character, but there are different ways in which this concern can be expressed. From this angle, the contrast between Dickens and George Eliot might be expressed as the difference between the externalised and the internalised novel. Dickens *implies* characterisation through the complex manipulation of externals, including a complicated plot. George Eliot, on the other hand, attempts to deal with her characters' inner lives more directly. From her point of view, a complicated plot would be a distraction that might take our attention away from what is her central interest, the spiritual and psychological lives of the people she creates. The fact that she does not primarily use plot to do this raises the question of what other techniques she has at her disposal.

Narration

This technique raises one of the central and interesting aspects of George Eliot's artistry. That is, how is the story told to us? Whose voice is speaking to us as the novel unfolds? There are many possibilities open to the novelist, each with its own attendant advantages and drawbacks. One method is that of first-person singular narration, the story being told to us by a character who has a part to play in the novel himself. This is an extremely vivid way of writing a novel, but it has the possible disadvantage of restricting the book's viewpoint to what can be seen, heard and guessed by one character. Alternatively, a novelist may choose an omniscient technique where he or she will have the freedom to explore all the novel's characters directly, a privilege that does not exist in real life.

As we can see from its opening, George Eliot intervenes very directly in *The Mill on the Floss* and this raises a problem of how we should describe the novel's narrative method. Should we simply say that it is George Eliot herself who is telling us the story? There are difficulties in this position, and a solution was suggested many years ago by a critic who argued that we should regard the narrator in a George Eliot novel not as the writer herself in a direct sense, but as what he called her 'second self'.* In other words, we should regard the narrator almost as a character in her own right, an ideal version of herself created by George Eliot with whom we can have a developing relationship as the novel progresses.

Something of what this means can be understood by examining a passage which refers to Maggie's childhood:

> Every one of those keen moments has left its trace, and lives in us still, but such traces have blent themselves irrecoverably with the firmer texture of our youth and manhood; and so it comes that we can look on at the troubles of our childhood with a smiling disbelief in the reality of their pain. (Book First, Chapter seven)

This passage is characteristic of George Eliot in many ways. It offers, as her novels so often do, a generalisation about the nature of human life. This fact raises the question of the status of such generalisations in a work of fiction, the assent or otherwise that we may give them. After all, a novel is not a philosophical treatise, and it might be thought that this kind of generalisation is out of place in it. For one thing, however, the intellectual content of George Eliot's observations is such that we are not often tempted to pit our wisdom against hers. But this question can also be dealt with more directly in terms of her artistry. If we felt that George Eliot's generalisations were being offered directly in her own voice, we might feel the kind of resistance to them that is possible in real life. After all, we are all tempted to feel that our ideas

*Wayne C. Booth, *The Rhetoric of Fiction*, University of Chicago Press, Chicago and London, 1961, p.71.

are just as good as the next man's. But with her use of 'us', 'our', 'we', and so on, we are drawn into a wisdom which seems to arise from the collective wisdom of humanity. Putting it another way, George Eliot is attempting to create the reader's ideal self just as she presents her own best self as the narrator.

We can see this in a brilliant passage that illustrates another, and more dramatic, use of narrative voice. This is the opening of Chapter two, Book Seventh where the narration takes on the collective voice of St Ogg's: 'If Miss Tulliver . . . had returned as Mrs Stephen Guest . . . bad as it might seem in Mrs Stephen Guest to admit the faintest advances from her cousin's lover . . . still she was very young . . . and . . . Guest so very fascinating.' In our own real daily lives we may be all too liable to judge as St Ogg's judges, but George Eliot is appealing to us to put aside this mediocre side of our characters (for life as well as art) in favour of a more compassionate view. However, this appeal is the reverse of a sentimental gesture towards our better selves. The passage begins with the statement that 'We judge others according to results; how else?—not knowing the process by which results are arrived at.' And it is precisely here that we can see one of the basic purposes of *The Mill on the Floss*, to make us understand the causes that lie behind the characters' actions, an understanding that is directly related to the novel's narrative method. For it is through George Eliot's constant analysis of motive that we come to understand her people so directly. This intimacy of insight would not be possible if we had to judge the characters purely dramatically; in other words, externally by their actions, dialogue and physical appearance. Early on in the book, Mr Tulliver goes to see his sister determined to insist on the repayment of some money that she owes him, but returns empty-handed and we find the following narrative comment:

And so the respectable miller returned along the Basset lanes rather more puzzled than before as to ways and means, but still with the sense of a danger escaped. It had come across his mind that if he were hard upon his sister, it might somehow tend to make Tom hard upon Maggie at some distant day, when her father was no longer there to take her part; for simple people, like our friend Mr Tulliver, are apt to clothe unimpeachable feelings in erroneous ideas, and this was his confused way of explaining to himself that his love and anxiety for 'the little wench' had given him a new sensibility towards his sister. (Book First: Chapter eight)

This depth of detailed understanding could only be given to us through narrative analysis.

Language

George Eliot has a much greater variety of prose than she is sometimes thought to possess. There is quite obviously a broad contrast between her narrative prose, for example, and her dialogue. As we might expect from the most intellectual of Victorian novelists, her passages of narrative analysis have a weight and gravity that can make them intellectually taxing, although the process of grappling with her intelligence can also have its own kind of exhileration. The following lines are merely an extract from the long passage dealing with Mr Riley's advice to Mr Tulliver about a tutor for Tom:

> Mr Riley was a man of business, and not cold towards his own interest, yet even he was more under the influence of small promptings than of far-sighted designs. He had no private understanding with the Rev Walter Stelling; on the contrary, he knew very little ... But he believed Mr Stelling to be an excellent classic ... Moreover, Mr Riley knew of no other schoolmaster whom he had any ground for recommending in preference ... His friend Tulliver had asked him for an opinion: it is always chilling in friendly intercourse, to say you have no opinion to give ... If you blame Mr Riley very severely for giving a recommendation on such slight grounds, I must say you are rather hard upon him. (Book First, Chapter three)

The entire passage does not make easy reading, but if we give it our full attention we can see that it is a masterly analysis of the way choices are very frequently made in our daily experience. And we may also understand a connection between the detail of the prose here and the novel's wider purposes. The book's moral insistence that we should try to understand one another more deeply is reflected in what might be called the sense of responsibility of the language. Its rather tortuous detail prevents us from moving quickly to any easy snap judgement and compels a slow working-out of the real complexities of human nature.

The weightiness of this kind of analysis is often lightened by a humour that George Eliot is sometimes mistakenly said not to possess, as when we are told that Tom's tutor believes in his educational system 'as a Swiss hotel-keeper believes in the beauty of the scenery around him, and in the pleasure it gives to artistic visitors.' (Book Second, Chapter one) But the sharpest contrast is provided by the earthiness of George Eliot's dialogue in the mouths of her humbler characters such as Bob Jakin or; higher up the social scale, the Dodsons. Aunt Pullet's constant harping on her neighbours' physical infirmities is particularly memorable. We can see the fusion here of two of George Eliot's literary influences, Sir Walter Scott and Wordsworth who both, in their different ways, gave an importance to members of social classes who had previously hardly appeared in English literature. By her own rich contribution George Eliot helped to make this interest into a tradition which she, in her turn, passed on to later novelists such as Thomas Hardy. When we hear Mr Tulliver telling his wife that she 'mustn't put a spoke i' the wheel' or that he won't be 'put off wi' spoon-meat afore I've lost my teeth' we are brought vividly into contact with characters whose language is directly related to their physical environment.

There is a connection between this earthiness and aspects of the novel's imagery, an imagery that makes its own special effect because it occurs relatively rarely in George Eliot's work, as when we are told of Mr Tulliver's attachment to the mill 'where life seemed like a familiar smooth-handled tool that the fingers clutch with loving ease.' (Book Third, chapter nine). This simile has the force of something almost tactile; in a real sense we can feel what Mr Tulliver's way of life meant to him. But as well as offering the reader isolated examples, George Eliot is also capable of deploying patterns of imagery, one of the most coherent examples of which is the use of the river in *The Mill on the Floss*. From first page to last the novel contains constant references to river, water and flood. These appear in dialogue as well as in the narrative, sometimes in ways that help to prepare us for the novel's climax, as when Mrs Tulliver complains 'They're such children for the water, mine are ... they'll be brought in dead and drownded some day.' (Book First, chapter ten). Indeed, this pattern of imagery is so strongly present that we may be justified in regarding it as symbolic although, as is the way with symbols, it may be possible to see more than one possible interpretation of it. A suggestion that does not seem to go too far is that the river may be a way of conveying the never-ending struggle of Maggie's inner self towards a higher life, a struggle which finally bursts its banks because of its uncontrollable frustration.

George Eliot's language is, then, a subtle and varied instrument, but it seems fair to end with the reminder that its overall effect is one of intellectual weight and moral seriousness.

Realism

The great Victorian novelists enjoyed a widespread popularity in their own time which has been the envy of modern serious writers. When George Eliot's first novel, *Adam Bede*, appeared in 1859 it 'became a sensational success, taking precedence over Dickens's *A Tale of Two*

Cities'*. Dickens was the dominating fictional presence of the age, but as his career developed there were signs that the sophisticated element in his public were becoming dissatisfied with aspects of his work. It was, above all, the melodramatic and sentimental side of Dickens, the grotesque and apparently exaggerated tone of his work, of which people were tiring. We can see now that these are not incidental blemishes, but are used creatively as part of his total artistic vision. For the nineteenth-century reader, however, there was something refreshingly new about passages like these:

> Mr Tulliver, you perceive, though nothing more than a superior miller and maltster, was as proud and obstinate as if he had been a very lofty personage, in whom such dispositions might be a source of . . . conspicuous, far-echoing tragedy . . . The pride and obstinacy of millers, and other insignificant people, whom you pass unnoticingly on the road every day, have their tragedy too; but it is of that unwept, hidden sort, that goes on from generation to generation, and leaves no record. (Book Third, chapter one)

We can see the force of Wordsworth's influence particularly strongly here in the respect that is given to the humble and inarticulate. What George Eliot adds is the psychological penetration that is so central to her greatness. Thus we are given not merely a shadowy outline of, say, Mr Tulliver's moral dignity, but an insight into his character which convinces us that he is just as humanly complex as the educated, articulate and sophisticated. It was this realism, this belief that the ordinary affairs of life demanded to be taken seriously, to which her first readers seem to have responded; it marked a fresh path for the English novel. That George Eliot was, from the beginning, self-consciously aware of what she was doing can be seen from a letter of defence to some criticisms raised by her publisher, John Blackwood:

> I am unable to alter anything in relation to the delineation or development of character, as my stories always grow out of my psychological conception of the dramatis personae . . . My artistic bent is not at all to the presentation of eminently irreproachable characters, but to the presentation of mixed human beings in such a way as to call forth tolerant judgement, pity, and sympathy. And I cannot stir a step aside from what I *feel* to be *true* in character.†

There is a danger of confusion in using the word realism about this aspect of George Eliot's work because of the cluster of meanings that

*Gordon S. Haight, *George Eliot A Biography*, Clarendon Press, Oxford, 1968, p.279.
†ibid, p.222.

exist around that difficult critical term. Her novels are realistic in that they deal with the ordinary, the humble, the shades of grey instead of the morally black and white. But, to use a popular sense of the term, George Eliot is not realistic in finding everyday life, by definition, sordid and futile. She is constantly at pains to bring out the possibilities for heroism in mundane existence and the fact that these possibilities are so often frustrated makes life tragic rather than meaningless. For her, tragedy is not simply one of the privileges of aristocratic wealth, but part of the texture of life at every level. And the heroism which is another integral part of her vision of life has nothing to do with physical feats performed before admiring multitudes. Characteristically, it is to be found in the solitary and inward struggles of her major figures. The best example of all this, is, of course, Maggie Tulliver.

Characters

Maggie

In creating the character of Maggie, George Eliot is in some sense dealing with herself and this was something for which she seemed to be not fully ready at the beginning of her career. Her first novel, *Adam Bede*, had a man for its central figure and we can sense the effort of will-power and courage necessary for *The Mill on the Floss*, which touched on her own experience at so many points. Maggie is a full-scale portrait of what the novelist herself might have been without the advantages of economic security and early intellectual inspiration. Certainly, one of the mainsprings of Maggie's character is very close to an important aspect of George Eliot's inner life:

> When Maggie was not angry, she was as dependent on kind or cold words as a daisy in the sunshine or the cloud: the need of being loved would always subdue her, as, in the old days, it subdued her in the worm-eaten attic. (Book Sixth, chapter four)

Such emotional dependence might seem sentimental or undignified if we were not made to understand its roots in Maggie's early life. Verbal language is usually taken to be the distinguishing feature of our humanity but, following Wordsworth, George Eliot might well have agreed that memory comes next in importance. If we ask what it is that makes our lives human, what above all gives us a sense of ourselves as coherent individuals, then it seems as if memory is a key factor by enabling us to connect one moment of our lives with another instead of living in a series of isolated sense impressions. Certainly, George Eliot's most positive characters are those that have this quality developed to a high degree as we see in Maggie's 'explanation' to Philip of his charge that she could never love him as much as Tom:

> 'Perhaps not,' said Maggie, simply; 'but then, you know, the first thing I ever remember in my life is standing with Tom by the side of the Floss, while he held my hand: everything before that is dark to me.' (Book Fifth, chapter one)

With complete psychological plausibility, Maggie's relationship with Tom as a little girl has become an indelible part of her adult personality, not merely in her continuing love for Tom, but in her need for love itself. This need is inextricably bound up with another trait to compose the foundations of her character:

> Maggie ... was a creature full of eager, passionate longings for all that was beautiful and glad; thirsty for all knowledge; with an ear straining after dreamy music that died away and would not come near to her; with a blind, unconscious yearning for something that would link together the wonderful impressions of this mysterious life, and give her soul a sense of home in it. (Book Third, chapter five)

Maggie is struggling here to unite two aspects of her experience that are in conflict: her belief in, and need for, a life of beauty and culture, of spiritual satisfaction, and her perception of the reality of ordinary life in St Ogg's. Maggie wishes to fuse her inner life with the external, to feel at home in both, but there seems nothing in St Ogg's that can satisfy this desire. In a way entirely characteristic of George Eliot, Maggie's character is related to the wider world about her. One aspect of this relationship is of special importance:

> Poor child ... she was as lonely in her trouble as if she had been the only girl in the civilised world of that day who had come out of her school-life with a soul untrained for inevitable struggles—with no other part of her inherited share in the hard-won treasures of thought ... than stretches and patches of feeble literature and false history. (Book Fourth, chapter three)

In other words, part of Maggie's dilemma is specifically related to her situation as a girl in Victorian England. As such, she is allowed only the almost frivolous education that was thought generally suitable for girls at the time and, apart from marriage, she cannot look forward to any widening of her social and personal sphere. (It is only under the stress of poverty that she succeeds in her insistence on being allowed to earn her living as a governess.) George Eliot herself escaped many of these disadvantages, at least partly through her own determined efforts, but it is worth noticing that she adopted a male pseudonym as a way of hiding her identity from the reading public, and one motive for this must surely have been the belief that her work stood a chance of being taken more seriously if it appeared to be written by a man.

Maggie's unconscious solution to her problems, following her reading of Thomas à Kempis, is the self-sacrificial attempt to deny her need for happiness and personal fulfilment. Her ultimate failure stems from the fact that this involves a kind of self-destruction, the rejection of aspects of her personality that are too vital to her life to be cast aside. The conflicts and tensions which this engenders can be seen throughout the novel, in her relations with Philip, for example. Philip goes some real way in the direction of opening out a world of art and beauty to Maggie, but George Eliot subtly indicates that there is something missing for Maggie in their contact:

> Maggie smiled, with glistening tears, and then stooped her tall head to kiss the pale face that was full of pleading, timid love—like a woman's.
> She had a moment of real happiness then—a moment of belief that, if there were sacrifice in this love, it was all the richer and more satisfying. (Book Fifth, chapter four)

Her happiness is only momentary, we notice, partly because she is being submitted to and one of Maggie's deepest personal needs is to be emotionally submissive herself. And after Tom's brutal separation of them she asks herself a strange question:

> And yet, how was it that she was now and then conscious of a certain dim background of relief in the forced separation from Philip? Surely it was only because the sense of deliverance from concealment was welcome at any cost. (Book Fifth, chapter five)

Do we really accept Maggie's explanation? Is it not, rather, that at the deepest level she does not love Philip, fond and grateful towards him as she is? Maggie is a strongly sensuous girl and unconsciously desires a sexual fulfilment that would not be possible for *her* because of poor Philip's physical deformity.

Tom

Maggie's brother is conscientious, hard-working and full of integrity, but his character is marred by two serious faults both of which are seen in him from his boyhood. He is self-righteously sure of his own goodness and completely lacking in what might be called moral imagination. He is blind to his own faults and at the same time unable to conceive of other ways of behaving than his own. This produces the mental attitude that George Eliot is most concerned to warn her readers against, a lack of compassion for the mistakes of others. We pity Tom for the sufferings he undergoes during his hopelessly unsuitable education, but are repelled by his thoughtless treatment of Philip at school. He appears at his best in his response to his father's downfall, as Maggie recognises at the moment when her father learns that his debts are to be repaid:

> Tom never lived to taste another moment so delicious as that; and Maggie couldn't help forgetting her own grievances. Tom *was* good; and in the sweet humility that springs in us all in moments of true admiration and gratitude, she felt that the faults he had to pardon in her had never been redeemed, as his faults were. (Book Fifth, chapter six)

But despite this, his emotional harshness and moral blindness continue until the end of the novel when, under the stress of facing death together with Maggie, Tom has 'a new revelation . . . of the depths in life, that had lain beyond his vision which he had fancied so keen and clear.' (Book Seventh, chapter five)

The Dodsons

The Dodson sisters represent what might be called the sociological side of George Eliot's genius. Although skilfully differentiated from each other, they are not presented in any psychological detail. They are best seen as a unit which embodies the writer's view of a significant segment of Victorian society. The sociological impulse at work here has nothing abstract about it. It is earthy, humorous and, above all, filled with concrete details which give us a complete picture of a way of life:

> There were particular ways of doing everything in that family: particular ways of bleaching the linen, of making the cowslip wine, curing the hams, and keeping the bottled gooseberries . . . Funerals were always conducted with peculiar propriety in the Dodson family . . . When one of the family was in trouble or in sickness, all the rest went to visit the unfortunate member, usually at the same time, and did not shrink from uttering the most disagreeable truths that correct family feeling dictated. (Book First, chapter eight)

George Eliot, however, is concerned with something more than external detail in this collective family portrait. She strives to penetrate to its inner reality and in some ways this makes for a depressing view of ordinary human existence. What the Dodson way of life lacks is any dimension of spirituality or intensity. Its materialism is so profound that it seems to be the only element within which these characters can live, although George Eliot is careful to point out that they have their own strongly held moral views:

> A Dodson would not be taxed with the omission of anything ... such as, obedience to parents, faithfulness to kindred, industry, rigid honesty, thrift ... the production of first-rate commodities for the market, and the general preference for whatever was home-made ... To be honest and poor was never a Dodson motto, still less to seem rich though being poor; rather, the family badge was to be honest and rich; and not only rich, but richer than was supposed. (Book Fourth, chapter one)

This, then, is the world within which Maggie has to live and we can feel how it could suffocate her aspirations for a wider life. But although George Eliot does not surprise us by sudden turns and twists in her plot, she can do so by the revelations that arise from her painstaking psychological analysis. When Maggie is at her lowest point it is Aunt Glegg, the most inflexibly rigid of the Dodsons, who offers to take her in:

> Mrs Glegg allowed that Maggie ought to be punished—she was not a woman to deny that—she knew what conduct was; but punished in proportion to the misdeeds proved against her, not to those which were cast upon her by people outside her own family, who might wish to show that their own kin were better. (Book Seventh, chapter three)

And so, in a way entirely characteristic of George Eliot's genius, we are made to admit the mixture of good and bad in the Dodsons as well as all her other characters.

Philip

The fate of this character forces us to recognise the sheer inequality and unfairness of human life. Philip's intelligence and sensitive appreciation of beauty enable him to give Maggie at least some access to the higher life for which she has been longing, but he is forever cut off from the fulfilment of normal experience because of his deformity. It would obviously be some consolation to him if he could be a real artist but, as he himself recognises, his gifts are those of the talented amateur.

This lack of sentimentality is carried through in the general presentation of his character where we see the faults that arise from his abnormality, his morbid sensitivity, bad temper and, above all, the jealousy that overwhelms him at the sight of Maggie and Stephen together. But the vein of nobility in his character emerges strongly at the end in the letter he writes to Maggie telling her of how his love prevented him from killing himself:

> Maggie, that is a proof of what I write now to assure you of—that no anguish I have had to bear on your account has been too heavy a price to pay for the new life into which I have entered in loving you. (Book Seventh, chapter three)

Stephen

Stephen is the conventionally attractive young man of Victorian literature. This raises the question of how suitable he is for Maggie. He is handsome, gay, charming, but George Eliot is careful to show us the connection between these personal qualities and his economic position in society:

> The fine young man who is leaning from his chair to snap the scissors in the extremely abbreviated face of the 'King Charles' lying on the young lady's feet, is no other than Mr Stephen Guest whose diamond ring, attar of roses, and air of *nonchalant* leisure, at twelve o'clock in the day, are the graceful and odoriferous result of the largest oil-mill and the most extensive wharf in St Ogg's. (Book Sixth, chapter one)

Conventional as he may seem, Stephen is a quite different type from the odius 'young Torry'. He is an enthusiastic singer, well educated and has a gentleness that is more than merely polite. Above all, his passion for Maggie is genuinely intense; it is far removed from the woman-hunting of any idle young rake. Stephen is perhaps surprised into his love for Maggie, not simply because of her unexpected beauty but because of an attitude of mind that leads him to patronise women:

> Was not Stephen Guest right in his decided opinion that this slim maiden of eighteen was quite the sort of wife a man would not be likely to repent of marrying—a woman who was loving and thoughtful for other women ... Perhaps the emphasis of his admiration did not fall precisely on this rarest quality in her—perhaps he approved his own choice because she did not strike him as a remarkable rarity. A man likes his wife to be pretty, but not to a maddening extent ...

> besides, he had had to defy and overcome a slight unwillingness and disappointment in his father and sisters—a circumstance which gives a young man an agreeable consciousness of his own dignity ... He meant to choose Lucy: she was a little darling, and exactly the sort of woman he had always most admired. (Book Sixth, chapter one)

We can see here that, despite his personal cultivation, Stephen is in his own way a product of St Ogg's. That is, in even such an intimate matter as the choice of a wife, he is partly governed by conventional considerations, although Lucy is in fact less conventional than he thinks. She seems to Stephen what is socially approved of in a wife and yet he is also able to flatter his vanity that he has chosen her. If he were less conventional himself, he might have been less vulnerable to Maggie's directness but, in fact, he has no defence in face of her honest rejection of feminine wiles.

Lucy

Lucy highlights the problems involved in the creation of a good character. We feel that she is pretty, lively and charming, but she fails to come alive to the imagination and perhaps the main reason for this is that she lies outside the area of George Eliot's 'artistic bent' which is the 'presentation of mixed human beings'.* Because of her age, inexperience and, especially her role in the novel, Lucy is not permitted the degree of complexity which makes the other major characters seem real to us. Of course, George Eliot's skill is too great to allow her character to remain at the level of a sentimental doll. She is humanised by little touches of humour in her treatment, as at this moment when Stephen has just left her:

> You will not, I hope, consider it an indication of vanity predominating over more tender impulses, that she just glanced in the chimney-glass as her walk brought her near it. The desire to know that one has not looked an absolute fright during a few hours of conversation, may be construed as lying within the bounds of a laudable benevolent consideration for others. (Book Sixth, chapter one)

And there is a hint of growing depths in her at the very end, in her last talk with Maggie when she says to her, 'in a low voice, that had the solemnity of confession in it, "you are better than I am. I can't ..."' (Book Seventh, chapter four). But Lucy remains, finally, a somewhat sketchy figure.

*Gordon S. Haight, *George Eliot, A Biography*, 1968, p.222.

Mr and Mrs Tulliver

The sheeplike Mrs Tulliver can hardly be said to possess such a human attribute as a character. Her bleating at the, for her, incomprehensible loss of her possessions may evoke some response from us, although it is hard to dignify this with such terms as pity and compassion. But we are shown, in a frightening way, that even the Mrs Tullivers of this world have wills and ideas of their own, when she decides to act for herself in seeing Wakem and thereby ruins the scheme for keeping Mr Tulliver on as manager of the mill. Her husband, with all his limitations, possesses the dignity of complexity as we see him struggling with the problems of a world that is to him mysterious. Unlike Uncle Deane, he has not adjusted to the changing conditions of his age and he finds questions such as how to educate Tom hopelessly difficult. But there is something lovable in a man who cares for his daughter and sister as he does and his final collapse is painfully moving.

Bob Jakin

Bob helps to illustrate the fact that sheer story-telling is not George Eliot's strong point, for he is brought in and out of the book somewhat mechanically as a way of advancing the narrative. But George Eliot's use of the rural dialect that she knew so well helps to give him a lively presence throughout the novel as in his description of how he earned ten guineas by putting out a fire or the use of vivid imagery to evoke the feel of his life. He explains his giving up the life of a barge-man, for example, by saying that ' "I'm clean tired out wi't, for it pulls the days out till they're as long as pigs' chitterlings." ' (Book Third, chapter six). Bob is clearly more than a little in love with Maggie, although he seems to worship her more as a lady than love her as a woman. Any possibility of his being a candidate for her is removed by his marriage.

Theme and meaning

The understanding of a fine work of literature requires imagination and sensitivity. Works of art are complex and subtle structures and there is no easy way of finding a key that will unlock every last significance to us. The text itself is, of course, the primary evidence for its own meaning, and we must be as attentive to it as possible. But we can see the text as embedded in a context of information: about the author's life, his or her other works, the work's place in literary history, the social history and ideas of its time, and so on. It is crucial not to allow any of this to take precedence over the text itself, but, if handled with discretion, such material can be useful in helping us to understand the work more deeply than might otherwise be possible. There are perhaps two major thematic centres to *The Mill on the Floss*, that concerned with Maggie herself and that which deals with the relationship between her and Stephen. Much of the reader's interest in Maggie stems from the conflict in her between aspirations towards spiritual beauty and the desire for earthly happiness. She constantly hopes to fuse these elements of human life into a wholeness and the frustration of these hopes reveals an important social dimension to her problems. St Ogg's has no place for the culture and passion that mean so much to Maggie and therefore a second aspect of conflict is brought out, that between the individual and his environment. Another social dimension to Maggie's difficulties is created through her hunger for education. Despite her parents' pride in her childish cleverness, Maggie is given only the education that was considered appropriate to the young lady of the period and thus her potential for self-development is cruelly stunted. The influence of environment extends even to the shortage of young men capable of appreciating an unusual girl like Maggie. The limitations of the provincial life depicted by the novel are such that it is only the crippled Philip and the culturally superficial, if attractive, Stephen who can see something of what Maggie is, or might be. In formal terms, these characters embody the tension in Maggie's desires between, putting it crudely, spiritual and sensual fulfilment. Each of them can give her only a part of what she unconsciously feels is necessary for a full life and, as a result, she is unable to give herself fully to either.

Maggie's inability to surrender herself to Stephen does, however, have other aspects and this takes us on to another major thematic centre of the book. We have seen that George Eliot underwent a crisis of religious faith that was in some ways representative of its period. The experiences of genius are, no doubt, felt more deeply than those of most of us and George Eliot followed their implications through with an unusual intellectual integrity. It is also probably true to say that a majority of Victorians remained convinced Christians. But a shift in certainty had taken place, thereby precipitating a process that has continued into our own time. For fundamentalist Christianity moral problems have a certain clarity, however great the temptation to evil itself may be. The Ten Commandments represent a sure guide to conduct as long as they are confidently thought to be the word of God. But as soon as this confidence slackens, if only by a little, the way is open to moral relativism, to the confusion that can result from the weakening of apparently objective standards.

George Eliot never avowed her loss of faith in her novels, neither out of cowardice nor with an eye to sales, but because she felt too strongly the responsibility of her position as one of what have been called the Victorian Sages.* Because of the doubts cast on Christianity by some aspects of contemporary thought, the Victorian public almost came to venerate its great writers as sources of wisdom and spiritual comfort. It turned to Carlyle, Tennyson, Dickens in this way and no less to George Eliot. The memory of her own joy in religious belief and the agony of giving it up remained too strong for George Eliot even to contemplate being the cause of a similar upheaval for others. For her it would have seemed the ultimate in arrogance to rob others of their peace of mind. She could not accept Christianity intellectually, but she retained too much awe in the face of the mysteries of the universe to believe that intellectual dissatisfaction should take precedence over human compassion.

Despite her rejection of Christianity, George Eliot remained deeply moral both as a woman and a writer. In fact, the suffering associated with her rejection of Victorian conventions made her, if anything, excessively occupied with questions of human behaviour. She and Lewes knew that their life together was at the furthest possible remove from that of the married lover with his kept mistress, but that is exactly how it appeared to an unsympathetic outside world. We can see, then, that in her own experience George Eliot lived through one of the central dilemmas of her time: what can justify the abandonment of what had previously been thought of as social laws rooted in God-given commandments. *The Mill on the Floss* is, on one level, a working out of this problem and it is significant that George Eliot felt the need to tackle it as early as her second novel. Without a solution to it her career as a writer might not have been possible.

The dilemma is faced head-on in chapter fourteen of Book Sixth in a series of exchanges between Maggie and Stephen that need to be quoted at some length. Stephen has allowed their boat to drift past its rendezvous with Lucy and Maggie tacitly acquiesces: 'she was being lulled to sleep with that soft stream still flowing over her, with those delicious visions melting and fading like the wondrous aerial land of the west.' (Book Sixth, chapter thirteen) But the next chapter is called 'Waking' and in it Maggie refuses to run away to be married:

> 'We have proved that it was impossible to keep our resolutions. We have proved that the feeling which draws us towards each other is too strong to be overcome: that natural law surmounts every other; we can't help what it clashes with.'

*See John Holloway, *The Victorian Sage*, Anchor Books, London, 1953.

'It is not so, Stephen—I'm quite sure that is wrong. I have tried to think it again and again; but I see, if we judged in that way, there would be a warrant for all treachery and cruelty—we should justify breaking the most sacred ties that can ever be formed on earth. If the past is not to bind us, where can duty lie? We should have no law but the inclination of the moment.'

We can notice the stress on law here: for Stephen the 'natural law' should take precedence over all others, while Maggie is fearful that this represents the triumph of momentary impulse. Both of them, in their different ways, feel that a law, some rule of conduct, is indispensible to the justification of their behaviour but it is noteworthy that Maggie does not fall back on the religious sanction as the answer to their dilemma. Her answer is, in fact, one that draws together and crystallises a dominant motif that runs throughout the novel. We have seen that a nostalgic preoccupation with the past was a widespread Victorian response to the unpleasant features of contemporary life and also that George Eliot herself had a deep emotional commitment to her own childhood. Both points can help to explain the role played by the past in *The Mill on the Floss*. The novel is indeed saturated in feelings of memory and time. Nostalgia is, however, a dangerous emotion, in life as well as art, and can lead to a merely sentimental fixation on old times for their own sake. George Eliot's intellectual power helps her to avoid this trap. Without any lessening of its emotional force, she is able to use the past for a coherent thematic purpose so that when Maggie cries 'If the past is not to bind us, where can duty lie?' we reach a climax that has arisen naturally out of a mass of earlier detail in the book.

There is something of the nature of a debate between Maggie and Stephen at this point, effectively dramatised as the exchange is. Its resolution was momentous for George Eliot's career and possibly also for us as inhabitants of a far more secular world than the Victorian one. The twentieth-century solution to this problem has been largely in terms of personal relations, above all in sexual love, and we can see this anticipated by Stephen later in the chapter:

'If you love me, you are mine. Who can have so great a claim on you as I have? My life is bound up in your love. There is nothing in the past that can annul our right to each other: it is the first time that we have either of us loved with our whole heart and soul.'

Again, Maggie's reply is in terms of the past, a past which is not visualised as merely neutral but as full of moral significance:

'There are memories, and affections, and longings after perfect goodness, that have such a strong hold on me . . . I have caused sorrow already—I know—I feel it; but I have never deliberately consented to it: I have never said, "They shall suffer, that I may have joy." '

The moral force of the past stems from the fact that through it our lives are inextricably bound up with those of others. Consent to the emotion of the present, however overwhelming, involves therefore a kind of self-destruction if it will cause pain to those who are close to us. We can see, then, that Maggie's agonised rejection of Stephen is of more than purely personal interest. It represents George Eliot's attempt to formulate, in artistic terms, what might be called a secular commandment, a guide to moral behaviour that is rooted in the daily experience of ordinary people. From this it follows that the meaning of a fine novel is not something self-contained, locked within an artistic object that has no relation to external reality. Works of art are not propaganda, but they are artistic statements about aspects of human life and, as such, are a vital part of real experience. George Eliot attempts to create a relationship between the narrator of *The Mill on the Floss* and us, the readers. This is an effective artistic device, but works at a level above the narrowly technical. It is, crucially, a mode of communicating wisdom about human life.

If we think about the novel in this way, especially in relation to Maggie's rejection of Stephen, we are forced to consider the book's ending. Why are we not permitted to see Maggie living through the consequences of her decision? This question has given rise to controversy amongst critics of *The Mill on the Floss*; the following comment by F.R. Leavis is an influential expression of a widespread dissatisfaction:

It is only the dreamed-of perfect accident that gives us the opportunity for the dreamed-of heroic act—the act that shall vindicate us against a harshly misjudging world, bring emotional fulfilment and (in others) changes of heart, and provide a gloriously tragic curtain.*

The verdict here is that by finishing the book as she does, George Eliot is guilty of wish-fulfilment and sentimentality. There is also the implication, and again it is a common view, that the novel's conclusion was some kind of afterthought. It is quite easy to dispose of this idea for a scholar has assembled the facts which show that the 'flood that ends *The Mill on the Floss* was not an afterthought to extricate the author from an impossible situation, but the part of the story that George Eliot

*F.R. Leavis, *The Great Tradition*, Penguin Books, Harmondsworth, 1962, p.58.

planned first.'* The internal evidence of the novel itself supports this view, as the commentary in this book brings out. From the opening pages there are clear indications of what the ultimate climax is to be. However, the fact that George Eliot had her ending in mind from the beginning does not necessarily imply anything about its value. Is it possible to take a more positive view than Leavis and other critics? One can only offer a personal opinion of certain aspects of this problem. Judgements of such matters as day-dreaming and sentimentality are so subjective that each reader must strive to reach his own viewpoint. But it does seem reasonable to suggest that the novel's climax can be seen to be related to the book's theme. When Maggie drowns in Tom's arms the novel seems to come full circle, in a way that is psychologically and thematically plausible, from the time when they stood 'by the side of the Floss, while he held my hand'. (Book Fifth, chapter one) Tom is the living embodiment of the rootedness of Maggie's life, of her place in an interconnecting web of human existence and, as such, he is the inevitable starting and finishing point of her life. We may find something rather limiting about this emotional dependence, but we can also see it as another element in the tragic pattern of poor Maggie's life. She may, in some ways, be too strongly bound by the past. But if this is so it can make her death seem all the more pitifully appropriate.

*Gordon S. Haight, in his edition of *The Mill on the Floss*, Riverside Edition, Houghton Mifflin Company, Boston, 1961, p.v.

Part 4

Hints for study

THERE ARE numerous practical methods that can be used for the detailed study of a novel. One is to become aware of the areas of debate concerning the writer or work one is studying, of the points at which disagreements arise. This section will concentrate on three of these areas which are relevant to *The Mill on the Floss* and to George Eliot in general.

Telling and showing

In the earlier years of the twentieth century, the Victorian literary convention of referring directly to the reader was frequently a topic for ridicule or, even, abuse. The basis of these objections was related to the techniques of such writers as Henry James and James Joyce, who sought to make their narrative as impersonal as possible by avoiding anything in the way of speaking to the reader or narrative analysis. Their aim was to make their work as dramatic as possible and the useful critical terms 'telling' and 'showing' have been developed to describe this difference. Critics of the Jamesian school felt that many Victorian novelists evaded the problems of art by telling their readers too directly and explicitly what was going on in their stories. The fault of this was thought to be that it rendered the reader passive: he had nothing to do but sit back and allow the novel to flow over him without the necessity of imaginative effort on his part. With showing, on the other hand, we are given scenes, characters and events directly, as we might see them in a play, and we are forced to interpret what is going on for ourselves because the writer will not tell us what to think or feel.

In *The Rhetoric of Fiction* (1961), Wayne C. Booth has helped to correct the imbalance of these earlier views by pointing out that telling has been an important fictional technique since the beginnings of the novel and that it can be a properly artistic device if its use is dictated by the work's overall purpose. He also demonstrates that the wrong use of showing can pose its own kind of difficulty. In other words, telling is not automatically bad and showing good; both have their own characteristic virtues and defects. Rather than blanket condemnation and praise, then, critical analysis demands that we discriminate between the good and bad uses of the two techniques.

George Eliot is a useful example here, because there are those who feel that, unlike, say, Dickens, she tells us altogether too much, especially at moments of climax when we should be left to experience the full impact of the situation dramatically for ourselves. Others will claim that authorial intervention is a crucial part of the artistic purpose of a book such as *The Mill on the Floss*. The novel's opening chapter is clearly relevant here and it might be useful to consider some of the opposing arguments that can arise from a representative passage:

> Ah, my arms are really benumbed. I have been pressing my elbows on the arms of my chair, and dreaming that I was standing on the bridge in front of Dorlcote Mill, as it looked one February afternoon many years ago. Before I dozed off, I was going to tell you what Mr and Mrs Tulliver were talking about, as they sat by the bright fire in the left-hand parlour, on that very afternoon I have been dreaming of.

The objections to such a passage are indicated by the rather extreme, but not unrepresentative, view of Ford Madox Ford, an English novelist writing in 1924:

> The object of the novelist is to keep the reader entirely oblivious of the fact that the author exists — even of the fact that he is reading a book. This is of course not possible to the bitter end, but a reader *can* be rendered very engrossed, and the nearer you can come to making him entirely insensitive to his surroundings, the more you will have succeeded.*

On this view, George Eliot's intervention will obviously be utterly inartistic. Instead of drawing us into an imaginary world without our being aware of it, as it were, she reminds us at the very beginning that we are reading a story which she is telling us. It might be suggested, on the other hand, that this is precisely the point of the literary technique which the writer is deliberately using here for artistic purposes. Given her interest in a certain kind of realism, in tracing the tragic potential of ordinary existence, it is crucial that she should establish a relationship with the reader which is similar to his relationships in real life. Ford Madox Ford's view might suggest that in some ways art is distinct from reality; for George Eliot art and reality are inseparable.

There is no easy answer to these complex questions. The great advantage of 'showing' is its intense vividness; of 'telling', its ability to

* Quoted from Miriam Allott, *Novelists on the Novel*, Routledge and Kegan Paul, London, 1965, p.273.

trace the depths of experience. The corresponding defects are an obscurity that stems from the author's unwillingness to guide our judgement and the boredom of pages of commentary rather than action. It would be a useful critical exercise to examine different kinds of narrative in *The Mill on the Floss* as a way of arriving at a personal estimate of these problems. We could make a specific comparison between the opening of Chapter one in Book Fourth and that of Chapter two of Book Seventh. Both are forms of narrative commentary, but they might be thought to be somewhat different in their effect and level of success. A basic question to ask about both would be their degree of relevance to their context and whether this relevance affects the element of narration in both passages in such a way as to dramatise it.

Language

Some of the problems involved in George Eliot's use of language are highlighted by the following passage from *The Mill on the Floss*:

> Already, at three o'clock, Kezia, the good-hearted, bad-tempered housemaid, who regarded all people that came to the sale as her personal enemies, the dirt on whose feet was of a peculiarly vile quality, had begun to scrub and swill with an energy much assisted by a continual low muttering against 'folks as came to buy up other folks's things,' and made light of 'scrazing' the tops of mahogany tables over which better folks than themselves had had to—suffer a waste of tissue through evaporation. (Book Third, Chapter six)

Two levels of George Eliot's style are present here: the colloquial and the 'correct'. There is plenty of earthy liveliness in the language that creates the little picture of Kezia with her scrubbing, swilling and muttering. The colloquial 'scrazing' is particularly forceful. This is a side of George Eliot that lent life and humour to her work throughout her career. It is richly present in the speech of Adam's mother in *Adam Bede* and in the rural and small-town choruses that we find in *Silas Marner* and *Middlemarch*. But there is an aspect of her humour and writing that has to be called heavy-handed. Of course, there is a comic intention in telling us in words the very opposite of Kezia's about the effect on her of hard polishing. But do we know what 'suffer a waste of tissue through evaporation' really means the first time we read it? Does it not take some thought before we realise that it means something like 'lose weight through sweating'? Of course, to point out this defect is only to say that George Eliot is not a perfect writer, but it remains a weakness nonetheless. We are prepared to read a sentence twice for the sake of one of her profound insights into human life, but it seems rather tiresome to have to do this in the case of a little joke.

We should not make too much of this; indeed, an earlier section of this book is devoted to bringing out the strengths of George Eliot's language. However, there is an area of disagreement here that we need to be aware of if we are to make a fully critical response to the novel. It has sometimes been suggested that the fact that George Eliot came so late to writing reveals that she is not a truly 'natural' novelist. We could add to this the claim that she is excessively intellectual and so construct a picture of George Eliot that would make her seem solemn, preoccupied with analytic commentary at the expense of dramatic embodiment and, worst of all, just plain dull. A clear example of these negative views may be found in the comments of Lord David Cecil from his *Early Victorian Novelists* of 1934:

> It is not just that she is not read, that her books stand on the shelves unopened. If people do read her, they do not enjoy her ... The virtues of her admiration, industry, self-restraint, conscientiousness, are drab, negative sort of virtues; they are school-teachers' virtues.*

We might wonder, in passing, what is wrong with school-teachers' virtues! However, from an historical point of view, it is true that this judgement is not untypical of a vein of George Eliot criticism that persisted through the latter part of the nineteenth century into the early years of the twentieth. On the other hand, a majority of critics would certainly agree with her biographer that George Eliot's reputation 'has now risen to the point where many authorities would place her again in the very top rank of English novelists'.†

Many of these disagreements have centred on differing responses to language and it is perhaps fair to remember that *The Mill on the Floss* is an early novel, a fact that may help to account for a certain unevenness of style in it. If this is so, it then becomes a useful work for testing our powers of critical discrimination. Can we distinguish between the different levels of style here and their relative degree of success? We may agree that the novel's use of colloquialisms gives it an earthy vitality which forms a useful contrast with Maggie's idealism. But are they sometimes overused, as with Bob Jakin in, for example, Book Third, Chapter six? Does this use of what are now unfamiliar words

---

*Quoted from *A Century of George Eliot Criticism*, edited by Gordon S. Haight, University Paperbacks, London, 1966, p.*XIV*.

†Quoted from *A Century of George Eliot Criticism*, edited by Gordon S. Haight, p.*XIV*.

impede the story's onward movement, instead of giving it the kind of raciness for which George Eliot was presumably hoping? Again, can we see the difference between passages where the novel's style is simply clumsy and those where it has a necessary weight and gravity? The content may help us here. The novel's speculations may sometimes seem a little banal; much more frequently, they have a depth which necessitates a certain complexity of language if they are to find full expression. Consider, for example, the meaning of the following passage and whether or not it is needlessly obscure:

> Not that Mr Wakem has not other sons besides Philip; but towards them he held only a chiaroscuro parentage, and provided for them in a grade of life duly beneath his own. (Book Third, Chapter seven)

We might compare with this the stylistic problems involved for the reader in the long section following Maggie's reading of Thomas à Kempis in Book Fourth, Chapter three.

Character identification

There is one area of alleged weakness that even George Eliot's greatest admirers have seemed unwilling to excuse her for and this is her supposed over-identification with her own characters, especially her heroes and heroines. Some interesting questions arise here about the nature of a novelist's attitude towards the figures he has himself created. It seems undeniable that many great writers seem to feel something like love for their characters; one thinks here of such figures as Shakespeare's Falstaff and Dickens's Mrs Gamp. Is it not, in fact, this love that explains the powerful emotional response in us towards them? But emotion must be balanced by objectivity for both writer and reader. We are incapable of learning anything from a character with whom we identify completely. Rather, we are simply being allowed, or taking for ourselves, the indulgence of sentimentality. Similarly, the writer must retain his power of dispassionate judgement if his character is to be something more than a self-projection, especially if the work contains autobiographical elements.

This helps to explain what F.R. Leavis means when he writes of 'the notorious scandal of Stephen Guest', the Stephen Guest 'who is universally recognised to be a sad lapse on George Eliot's part.'* Leavis is, in his turn, influenced by the views of the late-Victorian critic Leslie Stephen which are worth quoting at some length because of their incisive expression of what has become a widespread view:

*F.R. Leavis, *The Great Tradition*, p.52.

But when Maggie ceases to be the most fascinating child in fiction, and becomes the heroine of a novel, the falling off is grievous. The unlucky affair with Stephen Guest is simply indefensible. It may, indeed, be argued—and argued with plausibility—that it is true to nature; it is true, that is, that women of genius—and, indeed, other women—do not always show that taste in the selection of lovers which commends itself to the masculine mind. There is nothing contrary to experience in the supposition that the imagination of an impulsive girl may transfigure a very second-rate young tradesman into a lover worthy of her; but this does not excuse the author for sharing the illusion ... when she [Maggie] is made to act in this way, and the weakness is not duly emphasised, we are forced to suppose that George Eliot did not see what a poor creature she has really drawn ... If it was necessary to introduce a new lover, he should have been endowed with some qualities likely to attract Maggie's higher nature, instead of betraying his second-rate dandyism in every feature.*

We may feel that this is rather hard on Stephen while still agreeing that he is hardly the ideal partner for a girl of Maggie's distinction, but the important point at issue is whether or not George Eliot is aware of his deficiencies. The implication of this view, which has been taken up by other critics, is that Stephen represents some kind of fantasy fulfilment for a George Eliot who is still emotionally deprived despite her life with Lewes. In other words, she is *in* love with her character rather than simply loving him. There are complex psychological questions involved in all of this and we may wonder how they can be resolved in literary terms. One way to do this is to ask if we can see the novel as a whole taking any general attitude towards Stephen. Is it critical of him at any points or are we meant to give him our complete approval? This problem can only be dealt with, in its turn, by examining specific passages in some detail. What are we meant to think of Stephen at this point, for example?

The fine young man who is leaning down from his chair to snap the scissors in the extremely abbreviated face of the 'King Charles' lying on the young lady's feet, is no other than Mr Stephen Guest, whose diamond ring, attar of roses, and air of *nonchalant* leisure, at twelve o'clock in the day, are the graceful and odoriferous result of the largest oil-mill and the most extensive wharf in St Ogg's. (Book Sixth, Chapter one)

*Quoted from *A Century of George Eliot Criticism*, edited by Gordon S. Haight, p.144.

When Leavis says of the novel's heroine that 'Maggie Tulliver is essentially identical with the young Mary Ann Evans we all know'* he is suggesting the same weakness of subjective response in the author herself that we saw in the case of Stephen. Everything hinges here on the phrase 'essentially identical', for we may remember that Maggie's life is a tragic failure while George Eliot's was a success. Leavis is especially critical of the presentation of Maggie's aspirations towards a higher life and claims that this never 'acquires a sense of consciousness, learns to understand itself: Maggie remains quite naïve about its nature'.† This is, of course, true, but is it the same as saying that the writer is unaware of the mixture of motives in Maggie? We may feel that Maggie's inability to understand herself fully is part of her tragedy, related to the deficiencies of her education and environment. George Eliot could have written a much more autobiographical novel, but that would have been the success story of a most unusual woman, of a genius, in fact. Her subject was the frustration of noble impulses by a combination of personal weakness and unpropitious circumstances and we might see the absence of full self-knowledge as one of the ingredients of this.

What is at stake here is the extent to which we feel that the author is in command of her own work in all its implications. Is she imaginatively alive to the full complexity of Maggie's character and situation or are there elements in this of which she is unaware? Once again, we can use the method of referring closely to a specific passage, the moment when Maggie tells Lucy of her relationship with Philip:

> 'Yes, yes,' persisted Lucy: 'I can't help being hopeful about it. There is something romantic in it—out of the common way—just what everything that happens to you ought to be. And Philip will adore you like a husband in a fairy-tale. Oh, I shall puzzle my small brain to contrive some plot that will bring everybody into the right mind, so that you may marry Philip, when I marry—somebody else. Wouldn't that be a pretty ending to all my poor, poor Maggie's troubles?'
> Maggie tried to smile, but she shivered, as if she felt a sudden chill, (Book Sixth, Chapter three)

We are told nothing more at this point; we have to interpret the shiver for ourselves. It obviously reveals something of Maggie's growing feeling for Stephen but also, at a deeper level, a movement away from Philip. Maggie's unhappiness is, of course, connected to the frustration of her

*F.R. Leavis, *The Great Tradition*, p.52.
†ibid, p.55.

spiritual aspirations; however, we may also feel that it is part of a more ordinary kind of emotional deprivation. Maggie's need for love finds expression when she meets the first reasonably suitable man she has ever known. We may feel disappointed that Maggie sees love as the solution to all her problems, and with a man who does not seem entirely worthy of her, but can we feel sure that George Eliot is unaware of all this? Is it not, perhaps, a fully worked-out part of the total story of Maggie's life?

Part 5

Suggestions for further reading

The text

There are various editions of *The Mill on the Floss* in print at the moment of which the best is probably the Riverside Edition, edited by Gordon S. Haight, Houghton Mifflin Company, Boston, 1961.

Other works by George Eliot

The George Eliot Letters, edited by Gordon S. Haight, Oxford University Press, London, 1954.

Background reading

ALLOTT, MIRIAM: *Novelists on the Novel*, Routledge and Kegan Paul, London, 1965.

BOOTH, WAYNE C.: *The Rhetoric of Fiction*, University of Chicago Press, Chicago and London, 1961.

HAIGHT, GORDON S.: *George Eliot, A Biography*, The Clarendon Press, Oxford, 1968. This is the essential source for information about George Eliot's life.

HAIGHT, GORDON S.: *A Century of George Eliot Criticism*, University Paperbacks, London, 1966.

HARDY, BARBARA: *The Novels of George Eliot*, Athlone Press, London, 1959.

HARVEY, W.J.: *The Art of George Eliot*, Chatto & Windus, London, 1961.

HOLLOWAY, JOHN: *The Victorian Sage*, Archon Books, London, 1953.

LEAVIS, F.R.: *The Great Tradition*, London, 1948; Penguin Books, Harmondsworth, 1962.

The author of these notes

GRAHAME F. SMITH was educated at the Universities of Aberdeen and Cambridge. He has been an Assistant Professor of English at the University of California, Los Angeles, a lecturer at University College, Swansea and subsequently a lecturer at the University of Stirling where he is now a Senior Lecturer in English Studies.

As well as articles on nineteenth-century fiction and on the cinema Dr Smith has published *Dickens, Money and Society* (1968) and a study of *Bleak House* (1974) in the Studies in English Literature series. He is currently working on relations between the novel and aspects of society in the eighteenth and nineteenth centuries.

The first 250 titles

The first ten titles

YORK HANDBOOKS form a companion series to York Notes and are designed to meet the wider needs of students of English and related fields. Each volume is a compact study of a given subject area, written by an authority with experience in communicating the essential ideas to students of all levels.

AN INTRODUCTORY GUIDE TO ENGLISH LITERATURE
by MARTIN STEPHEN

PREPARING FOR EXAMINATIONS IN ENGLISH LITERATURE
by NEIL McEWAN

AN INTRODUCTION TO LITERARY CRITICISM
by RICHARD DUTTON

THE ENGLISH NOVEL
by IAN MILLIGAN

ENGLISH POETRY
by CLIVE T. PROBYN

STUDYING CHAUCER
by ELISABETH BREWER

STUDYING SHAKESPEARE
by MARTIN STEPHEN *and* PHILIP FRANKS

ENGLISH USAGE
by COLIN G. HEY

A DICTIONARY OF LITERARY TERMS
by MARTIN GRAY

READING THE SCREEN
An Introduction to Film Studies
by JOHN IZOD